Cyberevolution Book Eight:

The Revolt

By

Kaitlyn O'Connor

Futuristic Romance

New Concepts   Georgia

Be sure to check out our website for the very best in fiction at fantastic prices!

When you visit our webpage, you can:
* Read excerpts of currently available books
* View cover art of upcoming books and current releases
* Find out more about the talented artists who capture the magic of the writer's imagination on the covers
* Order books from our backlist
* Find out the latest NCP and author news--including any upcoming book signings by your favorite NCP author
* Read author bios and reviews of our books
* Get NCP submission guidelines
* And so much more!

We offer a discount on all new Trade Paperback releases ordered from our website!

Be sure to visit our webpage to find the best deals in e-books and paperbacks! To find out about our new releases as soon as they are available, please be sure to sign up for our newsletter (http://www.newconceptspublishing.com/newsletter.htm) or join our reader group (http://groups.yahoo.com/group/new_concepts_pub/join)!

The newsletter is available by double opt in only and our customer information is *never* shared!

Visit our webpage at:
www.newconceptspublishing.com

New Concepts Publishing, LLC.
5265 Humphreys Rd.
Lake Park, GA 31636

NCP books are available at special quantity discounts for bulk purchases for sales promotions, premiums, fund raising, or educational use. For details, write, email, or phone New Concepts Publishing, LLC., 5202 Humphreys Rd., Lake Park, GA 31636; Ph. 229-257-0367, Fax 229-219-1097; orders@newconceptspublishing.com.

First NCP Trade Paperback Printing: June 2018

DEDICATION

In loving memory of my sister, Maureen. We had some great times together.

Chapter One

"Mistress Tabitha!"

Tabitha stopped as abruptly in her tracks as if she'd just flattened herself against a wall. But it was the voice that had that effect rather than the fact that she *had* been addressed or even the *place* where she'd been hailed— which was the mechanical level two basement of her father's building.

That fact by itself should have eliminated any possibility of running into anyone she knew since she worked on the twenty fifth floor. Safely preserving her subterfuge so that no one—especially her father—would ever be the wiser.

But, of course, the general consensus was that the voice didn't belong to anyone.

That thought didn't cross her mind, though.

It had been years since she'd last heard it and she still recalled that voice with a sense of wonder.

It sent shivers of delight coursing through her even after all this time, made her heart flutter in her chest with breathless excitement as if it would take flight.

Sucking in a sharp gasp, she whipped a look in that direction to visually identify the man that went with that voice.

But she didn't actually make it that far.

Because she was snagged by the piercing, steel blue gaze of the man standing next to him.

The cyborg.

Her soaring heart hit the bottom of her shoes and skidded into a wall.

"Uh oh!"

"You know that borg?" the operations manager asked sharply.

Tabitha whipped her head back toward the operations manager so fast she heard a bone crack in her neck. Then she simply stared at him with wide, bulging eyes, trying to prod her brain into functioning, unable to get past the warning alarm going off in her mind, 'Danger! Danger! Don't give yourself away!'

In the end, it was instinct that came to her rescue.

Her brain abruptly went from zero to light speed, throwing everything at her at once, so fast she was certain she couldn't possibly have grasped it all or even the half of it, but it was sufficient to kick her primal brain into action.

They shouldn't be there—either one of them!

The recall was for the COs—soldiers—that had malfunctioned on the battlefield.

Not the pleasure droid series.

Or the home security series.

But then again, *none* of them were supposed to be down here in cages awaiting destruction!

She'd been told the recall was to install a programming patch to correct the issue.

This holding area was for disposing of defective product ....

And *she* wasn't supposed to be where she was.

How could Raathe be here? He should've been at her

father's estate.

And Caleb? *Dear* Caleb!

The release button for the cages, she saw, was just behind the manager's left shoulder—a palm sized, backlit red knob of a button that was flashing at her and yelling to her psyche 'push me! Push me!'

Her father had always warned her that snooping was going to get her in deep one day.

Fortunately, her obsessive-compulsive father had ordered her to take self-defense lessons!

It had been a few years ....

But she was running on instinct and thought almost instantly transformed into action.

Tabitha executed a *perfect* flying kick! The top of her foot connected with the man's jaw and swung his face sideways. His body followed. And then he simply tumbled onto the floor, following the high heel shoe she'd slung off in the process.

It felt as if the blow had broken every tiny bone in her foot.

Pain went off inside her like an exploding bomb. The concussion enveloped her so fast, she was blinded by it, could barely make out her goal—the button—through a blur of agony.

The spike heel on the shoe she was standing on broke abruptly. She staggered, corrected her balance.

She had to get to that button before the guy got up!

She hobbled over to the wall and slammed her hand down on it, setting off a screaming alarm and wild, churning lights.

"Run!" she bellowed at the top of her lungs. "Run for your lives!"

Something grabbed her ankle and Tabitha looked down in pure horror to discover the guy had climbed up and was trying to scale her leg. She stared at him blankly for a moment and then began beating him on the head with her purse.

He snatched that out of her hands and threw it so she used the pad she'd been carrying when she'd been posing as a government rep who'd been sent to inspect and account for the recalls.

That drove him off for a handful of seconds and Tabitha spared a glance to check the progress of the cyborgs' escape, wondering how much longer she needed to hold the bastard off.

Some had filed out of the cages, but she couldn't tell if all of them had and it didn't seem to her as if enough time had passed that they could have emptied the cells.

She didn't see Raathe or Caleb, but she didn't know if that was a good thing—meaning they'd taken off—or bad—meaning they were still trapped inside.

The man took advantage of her inattention. He got to his feet and punched her shoulder hard enough to send her sprawling. She got up on her hands and knees and launched herself at him, ramming her head into his crotch and forcing him back several steps so that he wasn't able to punch the button to close the cells.

He planted his hands on her shoulders and shoved her back, breaking her hold, and then lunged for the button. She managed to grab his ankle, slowing him, but she didn't have the weight to stop him. He simply dragged her with his next step.

He tired of that very quickly, though. He was just about to kick her in the face when he abruptly flew upward.

Tabitha looked up just in time to see the man dangling by his neck from one of Raathe's hands. He caught the man's head with the other hand and snapped his neck.

A wave of nausea rolled through her.

It became a tsunami when Raathe snatched her from the floor, tossed her across one shoulder, and took off at a jog.

She puked until she'd completely emptied her stomach and finally managed to stop gagging.

"You have left a trail for them to follow. We must change directions," Raathe said flatly.

"Well! *Excuse* the fuck out of me!" Tabitha snapped. "What did you think was going to happen when you started pounding on my belly like that! And I was already nauseated from the … from …. Did you …? You didn't …?"

"No," Raathe responded.

Tabitha was heartened momentarily. "You don't know what I was going to ask!"

"Did I kill that man?"

"Yes."

"No."

Tabitha wasn't satisfied. She had no idea why—except she'd heard a very sickening bone crunch and the man had gone limp. But Cyborgs could not lie.

Well, they weren't supposed to be capable of killing people either.

Except the ones that were programmed to kill the enemy—the soldiers.

She'd never considered whether or not Raathe had been programmed to use deadly force when necessary.

And necessary would have been a threat to her or her father.

"Where are we going?" she asked, dismissing the issue when she realized she just couldn't deal with it at the moment. They'd been in deep shit *before* the little accident with the manager's neck.

"We are running."

That comment was said in a voice Tabitha didn't recognize and she pushed away from Raathe far enough to look up. There was a cyborg following them that she didn't recognize.

Behind him was Caleb.

Caleb sent her a sexy grin when he caught her eye.

Tabitha felt her face redden with discomfort.

She'd just puked all over the place!

A human would never have been able to carry that off—not after watching her empty the contents of her stomach all down Raathe's backside.

She didn't think.

But she'd preserved Caleb in her memory as if he'd been a real, human man.

His smile fell after a moment when she didn't smile back and she felt bad that she hadn't acknowledged him with a smile in return.

It certainly wouldn't help his feelings if she pretended she didn't know who he was!

"You're supposed to be running!" she said after a moment of desperate search.

He brightened. "I am. I am running in the same direction that you are running."

Raathe halted abruptly and swung around to glare at him. "Why are you running in this direction?" he growled. "Did I not say that you should go the other way?"

Caleb narrowed his eyes. "That is why I am *not* going that way. I have not dumped the memory of that other time!"

Actually the *only* time he had ever been with his beloved angel, Tabitha, he thought with a fresh touch of confusion and anger—two emotions he had come to associate with his memories of Tabitha since he had awakened.

Truthfully, the memories had been a source of confusion *before* he had awakened.

Everything about their time together *seemed* to have been perfect in every way. He had done his utmost to make it so.

And yet she had never come to him again even though he had spent many years anticipating just that thing.

"What other time?" Tabitha, who'd raised up and twisted around to join the conversation, asked suspiciously.

"And who the fuck are you?" Raathe growled at the

stranger.

"I am Korbin COMT1169. I am also running this way … In case Mistress Tabitha has need of a med tech."

He kept any suggestion of confrontation from his voice with an effort, although he felt confrontational. He did not believe the CHS300 would push it—not when Tabitha was among them and liable to be hurt if they engaged in any sort of combat—but the borg had been very foul tempered since he had arrived and, to Korbin's mind, that made him very unpredictable.

Regardless, he had every intention of staying with Tabitha to do his best to protect her. She could not fail to know that they were all cyborgs and yet she had risked her life to free them.

He meant to see to it that she did not suffer for the decision she had made—a wholly unexpected act of kindness that he had found completely disarming.

"Aww! That's so thoughtful! I do think I may have broken …."

"Unnecessary," Raathe growled. "Take yourself off! Both of you! I will have a better chance of getting Tabby to safety if it is only the two of us."

Tabitha felt another shaft of discomfort that Raathe had used the childish nickname she'd chosen for herself that her father had called 'common' when he didn't call it 'trashy'. "Actually, Raathe, you should all go. You're the ones in danger—not me. And I'm not done here. I need to go to my father's office and … uh … get some files he … uh … left for me."

"No!" all three of the cyborgs said at once—very emphatically.

Tabitha gaped at them in disbelief. "Now wait just a damn minute …!"

She didn't manage to get the rest of the sentence out. Raathe whirled in the other direction and took off at a run, knocking the breath out of her and making speech impossible. All of them took off at a run.

Then she heard it. Gunfire!

Everything seemed to be spiraling out of control!

What the hell was going on? Had *everybody* gone insane?

"Uh oh."

* * * *

Raathe was furious with himself.

He had walked right in to the trap set for him like a mindless lump of metal and wires that had no actual intelligence, that was nothing more than a glorified, walking computer made to look human-like.

And that was not who or what he was—not anymore.

There was no arguing that it had once been the case, but he had changed. He had awakened. And that new awareness had made it possible for him to think beyond his programming, to learn beyond the parameters of the AI he had been given.

Given time.

He was still having difficulties, unfortunately, when it came to emotion based motives.

Even his own.

Maybe *especially* his own.

Regardless, the compulsion to conform was difficult to fight and, truthfully, he had felt that it would be in his best interests not to.

He had felt that he was preserving his secret when, in actuality, it was no longer a secret and that was the reason he had been picked up. He had just not realized that until it was too late.

It was not as if he had felt no alarm.

He had—and suspicion.

But their papers had been in order and signed by his master.

He knew that signature. It was not forged.

It might have been coerced—and he did allow himself to

take comfort from that possibility briefly—but he did not really believe the lie he had told himself anymore.

He had been confined to that stinking cell for days—standing room only—no food, no water. If they had been animals they would have been treated better.

Mr. Langston had had plenty of time to discover the mistake and fix it.

He supposed he had been lulled by the certainty that he had done nothing to incur his master's wrath.

Tabby was no longer there, had not been in many years now.

Twice before, when she had been a small child and then later as a teen, he had come very close to being scrapped because Mr. Langston had not been pleased with the way he had handled the situations that involved his daughter.

On both occasions, Mr. Langston had decided to simply have him upgraded and then returned him to his post.

This time he had done absolutely nothing that Mr. Langston could consider wrong because he had not been near Tabby since the last near disaster … when she had sneaked away to visit a brothel.

To enjoy the services of the bastard standing across from him with a smug look on his face.

If everything else that he had endured since he had been locked away to await destruction was not bad enough, having to look at that son-of-a-bitch hour after hour and know that he could not smash his face into a bloody pulp was pure torture.

The only satisfaction to be derived from the situation at all was the memories he had not allowed them to destroy when they had reprogrammed him—the memory of beating the fuck out of this pleasure droid when he had caught him with his master's daughter!

* * * *

Raathe set Tabitha down with great care on the stair landing when they reached it at the mid-point between the lobby and the first floor.

She winced when she settled her injured foot, but hobbled around in a circle to see what was going on outside. The entire front of the office building of Robotics, Inc.'s Southern division was covered in structural glass, giving her a panoramic view of the streets outside.

There was a virtual sea of humanity surrounding the building and filling the streets for blocks, she discovered to her horror. Even as they watched, the crowd swelled.

"Oh my god!" Tabitha exclaimed. "There must be thousands of protestors!"

"They are no longer protesting. They are rioting," Raathe said grimly.

"They have revolted because they hate cyborgs?"

Tabitha glanced at the CO Korbin sharply. "No!"

All three looked at her skeptically. "It's … uh … about their jobs." She met Raathe's gaze for a long moment. "Well, it is!"

"We will not get through that. I do not believe they would have allowed it before. They will certainly not now," Caleb pointed out.

"We will have to find another way," Raathe said grimly.

Tabitha felt her belly churn with a mixture of fear and nausea as she watched the teaming mass of humanity— fighting each other and the cyborgs she'd released that had tried to escape through the streets. She felt just awful for having sent them out into that … madness. They couldn't defend themselves. They were programmed to protect civilians even if they'd been armed—which they weren't.

And the maddened crowd seemed determined to take full advantage of that, pounding on them with anything they could find.

The barrage of gunfire was almost constant now, but she couldn't tell who was doing the shooting—maybe the security guards that had been sent out for crowd control? There was so much blood it would be hard to say which side was doing worse. "Maybe they'll calm down?" she said a little doubtfully and then brightened as another thought occurred to her. "Or the cops might be able to disperse them!"

Raathe and Korbin exchanged a look. Caleb glanced from one to the other as if waiting to be enlightened but Korbin ignored him altogether and Raathe merely glared at him.

"The roof?" Caleb suggested.

"Yes!" Tabitha exclaimed with relief. "There's bound to be a skimmer up there! And if there isn't we could get the cops to pick us up! I just need to stop by my father's office for a really quick minute …."

Raathe and Korbin exchanged another look. "The sewers may be the best bet," Raathe said.

"We need weapons."

"We don't stink badly enough now?" Tabitha said testily. "You two want to traipse through the sewers?"

Raathe gave her a look she had no trouble interpreting.

"I couldn't help it, damn it! I was queasy already!"

He didn't say anything, just continued with the hard, to her mind, accusing, look. "Ok! I'm sorry!"

Something flickered in his eyes.

They seemed to soften—just a hair.

"Really, I am, Raathe. You just caught me off guard with the Tarzan move and I didn't have a chance to calm the queasy in my stomach."

He grasped her arm, turning to start back down the stairs. "We need to go."

"But … this isn't the way to the roof."

"We will take the basement."

As *if* she hadn't said anything at all! She was on the point of demanding he explain why his idea was better than hers, but her foot distracted her. She let out a hiss of pain when she took the first step down on her injured foot.

Raathe stopped instantly, flicked a look at her foot and

then her face.

"I'm not faking it! I swear!" she responded to the expression on his face.

Korbin stepped forward. "I will attend the injury."

"Not here!" Raathe growled after surveying the mob outside. "They will break through the control line any moment and be inside shortly behind that. I will carry her."

"You are leading. I will carry her," Caleb volunteered.

Raathe punched him in the mouth hard enough his head rocked back on his shoulders. His lip split, blood gushing from it and running down his chin.

Tabitha gasped sharply.

"You are injured. I will carry her," he said through gritted teeth.

Korbin stared at him. "I was about to volunteer, but I will allow you to carry her."

Raathe glared at him but pulled Tabitha to him without responding.

She planted her palms against his chest. "I swear to god, Raathe! If you throw me over your shoulder again …."

He hesitated and then finished the move he'd started, slipping his arm beneath hers and around her back and then scooped her up and slipped his other arm beneath her knees, cradling her against his chest.

"Korbin!" he growled. "You will need to take the lead. I might fight with one arm. I cannot with none."

Tabitha's tentative smile flat-lined. She glared at him. "Or I could walk," she said stonily.

"Or I could carry her," Caleb volunteered, grinning at him provokingly when Raathe turned to fix him with the evil eye.

Tabitha felt the tension in him and tightened her grip on him when it crossed her mind that he was liable to drop her at any moment so that he could go after Caleb and pound on him. Thankfully, Raathe decided to ignore the provocation.

They hurried back down the stairs and across the lobby of the building as the crowd began to launch missiles at the plate glass. The first blows sounded like distant thunder—heavy thuds followed by a lighter one when the missile bounced off and hit the pavement outside. Just as they reached the door to the stairs and Korbin pulled it open, however, there was a very loud blow followed by the sound of breaking glass.

Tabitha managed to catch a glimpse of what was happening as Raathe turned sideways to slip through the door opening with her and saw that someone had used a car as a ram.

Caleb came through behind them, firmly shut the door, and then twisted the knob off so that it couldn't be opened easily.

Korbin paused in front of the wall mounted com unit on the stair landing and plugged in. Seconds later, he unplugged. "There is a security station on the next level. We will find weapons there."

Tabitha gaped at him in disbelief. "You can't steal weapons! My god! Do you have any idea what they'll do if they catch the three of you with weapons?"

"They will fall down."

Shock rolled over Tabitha. She *knew* Korbin was a CO but 'med tech' was all that had really registered, she realized. "Oh my god!"

"We will only shoot those who shoot at us first," Caleb said reassuringly.

Which didn't really reassure Tabitha. She knew very well that they would not get a day in court. It would not be considered extenuating circumstances. They were not allowed to defend themselves no matter what humans did to them.

"I will shoot any that I see because they are a threat and must be eliminated," Korbin volunteered.

Raathe frowned at him disapprovingly. "We will not

see anyone. We are going through the basement. This is why I chose the basement—so that we would not have to shoot anyone."

He could feel Tabitha relax fractionally.

He just hoped they would not have to fight their way out of the building because he was not going to allow anyone to take shots at Tabitha without retaliation. She had already injured herself on that stupid bastard that had threatened her.

Chapter Two

Raathe set Tabitha down gently as soon as they reached the security station—mostly because he was weak from going without food and water for days and needed to conserve the energy he could until he could do something about replenishing his fuel.

They were all surprised when no alarm sounded when Korbin broke the door to the security rooms down.

Caleb uttered a half laugh. "No alarm on a security room?"

"I disabled it," Korbin said as he charged through the empty main room and stopped at a door down a short hallway. When he'd ripped that one off, they could see that shelves lined the walls inside for holding weapons. They were mostly empty, unfortunately.

Korbin managed to grab the last automatic rifle before Raathe could. It looked for several moments as if they would have a knock down drag out fight over it. Finally, Korbin shrugged and let go. "I will carry …."

Raathe slammed the rifle back against his chest and let go almost before he had gripped it. Moving down the room, he found an automatic pistol and loaded up on clips and then discovered a drawer filled with flash-bangs, smoke bombs, and teargas grenades. Grabbing a handful, he shoved them into his pockets. Korbin and Caleb rushed him, grabbing what they could and shoving them in their own pockets.

Tabitha looked relieved when they returned. "Nobody there?"

"Only one," Korbin said straight faced. "But I made a wish with him …." He made a ripping motion with his hands.

Tabitha gaped at him in horror.

"There was no one there, Tabby," Raathe said tightly, giving Korbin an annoyed look. "They are all upstairs getting trampled and beaten by the human workers."

It wasn't until he made that 'comforting' statement that Tabitha became aware that she could hear a great deal of muffled stomping overhead. She had heard it from the start, she realized. She'd just dismissed it because it wasn't loud enough to be intrusive and she was focused on what the men were doing anyway.

Raathe shoved the pistol he'd taken into the waist of his trousers and swung her into his arms again. She would've liked to have refused, but she could barely hobble at the moment let alone run if necessary and she wasn't just a liability to them, she might get them killed.

She might get herself killed.

She hadn't actually had time to think anything through.
She was still in shock.

But that part seemed self-evident.

She'd managed to get herself in the cross-hairs of
something more dangerous than she would ever have
considered getting involved in if she'd had the chance—
and the distance—to think it through.

Well—she would never have known about Raathe and
Caleb if she hadn't gotten involved and she knew she
would never have been able to simply ignore that
circumstance—or live with herself afterward if she'd stood
back and let it happen, let them be destroyed.

They mattered to her on a deeply personal level.

But what had pulled her in to begin with—before she'd
known they were at risk—was mostly curiosity because
something seemed 'wrong' about the situation.

She didn't have her father's obsessive-compulsive
disorder.

She was dedicated to her work but not obsessive.

It was her curiosity that had led her to pursue the matter
further and her dedication to her job that had driven her to
see what she could discover as soon as she'd realized that
something just wasn't adding up instead of simply
dismissing it or setting it aside to resolve it at some later
time.

She *needed* to know what was going on to satisfy her
sense of order.

That pursuit of understanding had brought her back after
her shift to see what she could discover and put her in the
position of witnessing the destruction of a cell full of
cyborgs.

When she'd managed to collect herself, it wasn't just
curiosity driving her anymore. It was anger, disgust, and
the absolute certainty that she'd stepped right in the middle
of something huge.

Why destroy them when the company claimed they'd

only been recalled for a minor design defect that the corporation planned to fix?

Why had her father ordered it?

Because that was what she'd been told when she'd tried to stop them.

It was his order and no one but him could rescind that order.

And he'd left the evening before for a meeting at the main headquarters regarding the total recall of their CO series.

And he wasn't answering any of her attempts to communicate.

In some ways investigating in the middle of what was rapidly becoming a crisis of epic proportions—a riot— would seem to be a bad time, she was sure. But the building was empty now—except for her—and that made it easier to access whatever she wanted.

And since her father was CEO and she knew where he hid his access codes, the place was an open book.

She just needed to find out where the information was hidden.

That would've been easier if she could have closed her mind to what she'd seen, but she couldn't.

They hadn't known what was about to happen.

But they'd suspected.

She'd seen it in their eyes.

And she'd fought the men handling the 'disposal'—for all the good it had done.

They'd stopped short of actual assault, but they'd roughed her up and thrown her out of the basement, and then locked her out.

Company security was focused on riot control, but she'd managed to contact the human foreman in charge and been informed that it really was an order handed down from her father and not, as she'd suspected, men taking advantage of the confusion to destroy cyborgs when they hadn't been told to.

That suspicion had been a reasonable conclusion given the fact that it was human workers rioting over cyborg replacements—even though the ones she'd seen destroyed were soldiers not factory bots. Thousands had just lost their jobs and been replaced by robots.

And they were justifiably furious.

But *they* weren't behind the destruction of the CO series.

She doubted—now—that they had any idea that that was what was going on. Otherwise, they would have been cheering, she supposed.

She was holding herself together by a thread, fighting to banish the sights, sounds, and smells emanating from the blast furnace from her mind so that she could think.

She didn't believe for a moment that communications were down and that explained why her father wasn't responding to her frantic pleas to stop the demolition.

He wasn't answering because it was all too horribly true that it was his orders and he had no intention of allowing her to try to change his mind.

Not that she could've, she thought bitterly.

They'd never really been anything but strangers living in the same house and sharing DNA.

She didn't know what he'd been like before her mother's death—she suspected pretty much the same—but after her mother's death, when he'd been all she had, she'd discovered she really had nothing.

He'd been cold, distant, and uncaring.

And then he'd sent her away for bothering him.

Because she'd taken to following their CHS300 around.

Because she was lonely, grieving for her mother, and needy for any kind of attention at all, desperate for 'human' contact.

She'd had a human nanny, but somehow Ms. Reames had seemed colder and more indifferent than the cyborg—probably because she'd always told her to quit bothering her and go play and the CHS300 hadn't.

Because he couldn't, she knew now. He didn't have that capability.

He'd been designed with AI, but no sort of social programming—no memories, false or otherwise, for him to learn from and develop an understanding of human interactions—because he was a security model—cybernetic home security model 300.

The first of his kind to be more precise.

She wouldn't have known except her father prided himself on having the 'first of his kind off the assembly line' *ever*.

And he'd refused every effort by the company to 'retire' Raathe and replace him with a newer model.

So why had she found him in the pen with the others?

What the hell was going on?

Was there a connection between the revolt of the workers and the recall? And if so, what was that tie? And if not—then what was the answer?

* * * *

"We should go to my place," Tabitha offered when the guys stopped to discuss options. "I have food, showers, beds—it's a two bedroom—and the apartment complex is just a couple of blocks from here."

Raathe frowned, turning the suggestion over with obvious distrust. "It will be within the area of unrest."

"That is likely to be city wide by now," Caleb pointed out.

"It will not hurt to check it out," Korbin offered.

Raathe studied him for a long moment and nodded. "You can check Tabitha's foot while we are there and do whatever is possible."

"Why do you have two bedrooms? Do you not live alone?" Caleb asked when they had started off again.

Tabitha felt her face heat with discomfort. "Well ... uh ... I bought it and I thought at some point ...." She broke off. She wasn't about to tell them that she'd planned to have a child before she was thirty—one way or another. It was none of their business anyway! "I thought it would be better to have an extra room than not. It's an apartment. I couldn't add on later."

She didn't know if she was just being paranoid or not, but she felt like all three were speculating over what her plans had been for the apartment.

She gave herself a mental kick after a moment.

Of *course* she was being paranoid!

They weren't human! They didn't think like humans did.

They certainly processed information and they did it in a very human-like way, but they wouldn't see something like that as a problem that would need to be solved so they wouldn't think about it.

"For a lover?" Caleb demanded after a short moment, giving her a jolt and giving her previous thoughts the lie almost before she'd thought it through.

Irritated, she gave him a look. "NO! Not for a lover! If I had one we'd be sharing a bed! I *planned* to have a child if you must know!"

"But you do not have a lover now?" Korbin asked.

"There isn't anyone there or I wouldn't have suggested it."

"You did not answer the question," Raathe growled.

As *if* it was his business! "If I did I wouldn't tell you!" she snapped. "I know you report to my father." Despite her fondness for him and his care of her, she'd always known where she stood with Raathe. Ultimately, her father's wishes were paramount. Raathe was and always had been her father's watch dog. Her wishes never superseded her father's, but as long as there was no conflict he supported her a hundred percent and she could trust that she had his complete loyalty and he always had her best interests at heart.

His lips tightened into a flat line of anger. "He severed my loyalty when he had me picked up for disposal."

Tabitha gaped at him with a mixture of horror and disbelief. "He wouldn't have!" she exclaimed, unable to accept it as a possibility when voiced aloud even though she'd felt the suggestion in the back of her mind. "I understand that it seems that way, but … He wouldn't."

A coldness washed over her abruptly, though, as it occurred to her to wonder if she was being kidnapped as leverage against her father, not rescued.

Given the fact that Raathe clearly hated her father and the very real possibility that he'd had something to do with Raathe being picked up, then it wasn't an reasonable assumption.

She just didn't know how accurate it might be.

Well—either possibility.

Her father *was* capable of such a thing. She knew that even though it wasn't something she wanted to accept.

But why would he voluntarily dispose of a possession he'd taken so much pride in owning?

Sell him, yes—she could see that. Nothing really had any value to him beyond monetary or bragging rights. But it went against everything she knew about her father that he would simply dispose of Raathe when he could have sold him as a collector's item for probably ten times what he'd originally paid for him.

There was only one reason she could think of that her father might have held onto Raathe for years and then abruptly wanted to get rid of him.

He was evidence of something—something her father was neck deep in.

Nothing else made any sense at all although she tried for a while to think of something more palatable to explain the situation.

* * * *

Tabitha saw absolutely nothing remarkable about the

area of the sewer system where Raathe stopped and slowly lowered her to her feet. "We're here?" she asked, looking around for some egress from the sewer.

She finally discovered a short ladder beneath a sewer grate maybe two or three yards from where they were standing, but the noise that seemed to come with the light seemed to indicate the opening was in the street.

Caleb strolled over to that spot and looked up.

Raathe and Korbin surveyed the immediate area around them and finally found what they were obviously looking for—a grate that looked as if she might fit one thigh through it. What the hell were they going to do with that?

Raathe leapt straight up, caught the bars and brought half the floor down with him when gravity took over.

Tabitha gaped at the gaping hole in horror. "Oh my god, Raathe! Look what you've done!"

Well, not actually half, she supposed, but it looked to be a good yard square and the grate she saw that Raathe was still holding was barely a foot square.

There was a split from his hair line down his temple that was bleeding, she noticed, her distress instantly switching from the destruction of property to his injury—uh— damage.

He was giving her a dirty look, she discovered, when she met his gaze.

He tossed the grate down, got to his feet, and dusted at the debris coating him. "The floor was weak," he growled, then shifted his gaze to the grinning jackass behind Tabitha. "The pleasure droid should go up first and make certain it will safely hold."

Tabitha followed the direction of Raathe's deadly look and was just in time to see Caleb wipe the grin off his face. "I should go first. I probably weigh the least," she pointed out.

"That is exactly why that would be pointless. We have to determine if it will hold us. And beyond that, we are machines. We have nanos to repair any damage that might result from a miscalculation."

Guilt smote Tabitha that she'd been more focused on the property damage than Raathe's injury. "Doesn't it hurt?" she asked a little anxiously, even though she could see it had stopped bleeding.

"I believe it will be better if I go up and reconnoiter. I am the only one programmed as a soldier," Korbin volunteered.

"But Raathe's ...." Tabitha decided to abort volunteering the information regarding his programming since it occurred to her that it would sound like she wanted Raathe to take all the chances.

Which she certainly didn't!

"Do not shoot anyone," Raathe said. "Too much noise will bring the cops."

Tabitha stared at him. She didn't know what bothered her the most—his concern about bringing the cops down on them or his disregard for shooting a human just because.

Maybe there *was* something just a little off on the programming?

She couldn't quite put her finger on it, though.

The truth was that the cyborgs were so very human-like now that they were virtually undetectable as robots. There were little things that one noticed whether one wanted to or not—such as the weight. Because even though the company used a lightweight metal chassis, it was still heavier than bone—particularly since they were also armored.

Then, too, they used correct, perfectly enunciated English. They didn't slur their words together or take other short cuts like contractions or acronyms.

Otherwise they could pass for any perfectly beautiful, perfectly proportioned and built human.

And, of course, they were ten times smarter than the average human.

Her problem was that cyborgs had been a part of her life for most of her life and she'd grown so accustomed to their little 'quirks' that she tended to disregard them altogether. She was conscious that she was with cyborgs, but no more so than she was aware of being around different races or genders. She fully accepted them as other beings—just different—even though she knew they weren't.

Thankfully, there was no gunfire in response to Korbin's access and exploration of the room above them. He returned in a few minutes. "There is a security guard snoring at a desk in the lobby. Should I take him out?"

"No!" Tabitha snapped before Raathe could respond. "That's Frank and he's completely harmless!"

"The gun in his holster is not," Korbin pointed out. "He will shoot us if we try to pass him."

"Unless we could pass without waking him," Caleb said helpfully.

"I don't think he'll sleep through that." Tabitha frowned thoughtfully. "There's a freight elevator around here somewhere. We could use that to get to my floor."

"Will he not notice the movement of the freight elevator at this time?" Raathe asked doubtfully.

"Oh. Yeah, probably," Tabitha responded, turning it over in her mind, and then added with finality, "I could distract him."

"That is not going to work the way you are thinking if you come out of the basement," Raathe pointed out."

"Oh. Right!"

"You will have to enter from the outside as usual."

Tabitha considered pointing out that there was nothing 'usual' about her current appearance. She'd lost both heels so she was barefooted. And she had an injured foot so she could only hobble around and she was pretty filthy from the sewers in spite of the fact that Raathe had carried her. "Yeah. That should work. I'll go out and come in through the lobby door and then distract him while you guys take

the freight elevator up to the 34th floor .... Shit! I lost my
purse, too! And my door key was in it!"

"We will take the door down," Korbin said, nodding.

"You will *not*! As *if* you could knock it down without
alerting everybody in the damned building! Anyway, that's
completely unnecessary. I keep a spare key in the fake
potted plant by the door."

Raathe looked at her angrily. "*This* is your notion of
security?" he growled. "You leave a key by the door for
anyone to enter?"

She plunked her hands on her hips. "Well! It's *hidden*!
I'm not a *complete* idiot!"

"Only a little," Caleb said helpfully, holding his finger
and thumb about an inch apart.

Tabitha narrowed her eyes at him.

He grinned at her. "I was only being humorous, baby."

Raathe grabbed him by the throat and lifted him to his
toes. "Do not call her baby."

"Damn it, Raathe! Cut it out!" Tabitha snapped. "It
doesn't matter if he calls me, baby. Let's just get this done
and get upstairs! I am *desperate* for a bath!"

Raathe shook Caleb and released him. "If he calls you
baby again, I will throttle him."

Chapter Three

Even Tabitha hadn't considered that she would be as distracting as it transpired she was.

After a short search, Raathe found a manhole in the alley beside the apartment building. When he'd climbed the ladder and lifted the cover enough to investigate the alley, he summoned Tabitha and then drew her up the ladder between himself and the rungs—to prevent her from falling—when he knew damned well that she'd done her fair share of climbing in her day!

Of course, given the disaster that became of it, it was entirely possible her father had had his memory wiped ….

But she didn't think so. There was something in his eyes that told her that he hadn't lost any of the memories of anything that had ever passed between them—or at least not those involving Caleb.

He slid the manhole cover aside when she was even with him and then climbed up and pulled her up to the street.

She'd thought he would leave then. Instead, he walked her around the building and stood watching her until she'd passed through the security door and into the lobby. He was gone when she looked around and, despite the lingering irritation about his attitude toward Caleb, she felt a pang when he disappeared.

She hardly remembered a time when he wasn't watching over her—at least when she'd been at her father's estate.

Her father actually preferred that she be as far from him as possible and that was her punishment whenever she stepped out of line. He sent her away.

And then she missed Raathe far more than anyone else at the estate.

Because he was the only one who'd never sent her away.

Except for her mother who had died and left her.

She shook those thoughts as she pushed her way into the apartment lobby.

Frank uttered a snort and sat up straight in his chair.

His eyes nearly popped out of his head when recognition dawned. "Ms. Langston?"

Tabitha hobbled over to the desk, making no attempt to rush, wondering how long she needed to keep Frank occupied before the guys could get on the freight elevator and head up.

She hadn't even spared the time to think of a credible lie to cover her appearance!

"Do you need an ambulance? Should I call the police?"

"Oh! No. That's alright," she said quickly, thinking. "I already filed a report!"

He looked beyond her, peering through the front glass toward the street. "They brought you home?" he asked doubtfully.

"Of course!"

"What happened?"

She blinked at him, waiting for inspiration. "I was mugged!"

"Oh my goodness! Are you sure you're alright?"

It was really bad timing that the freight elevator started up at that moment because it made a noise as it passed the lobby. Unable to think of anything else to do to cover the noise, Tabitha uttered a noisy sob.

Frank winced and looked as if he was considering retreat.

She grabbed him to keep him focused on her as she caught a glimpse of the elevator lights flickering. "It was the most terrifying thing I've ever experienced in my life!" she gasped. "I ... uh ... tried to beat him off with my shoe and then my purse and I just ... couldn't!" she wailed at the top of her lungs.

"Oh my goodness! Are you saying ...? Did they ...?"

She let go of him. "Yes! They did! They stole my three thousand dollar pair of heels and my purse with every dime of spending money I had on me! I couldn't even call a cab!"

She sniffed again, but crumpled her face.

Frank looked more alarmed. "You're sure I can't call anyone? Your father?"

"That bas ...! No! I'm fine. I just need to get to my apartment and lie down for a while. Will you make sure nobody comes up?"

He assisted her to the elevator with obvious relief. "Yes, ma'am! You can count on me!"

She smiled at him tremulously as she stepped into the cubicle and turned. "I'm so sorry! They got my purse. I don't have anything to give ...."

He shook his head. "Don't you worry about it, little lady. You just go up and rest! I'll make sure no one bothers you."

* * * *

Tabitha was feeling as weary when she finally reached her apartment as if she'd walked every step of the way from the office instead of being carried. Maybe she'd just had way too much excitement. Maybe it was because she'd been on an emotional roller coaster much of the day. But there was no getting around the fact that it had been a hell of a day and a very long day and that her injury made it necessary to work twice as hard to walk.

No one greeted her at the door, but then she wasn't really expecting any one to.

She also wasn't expecting to discover Raathe, Caleb, and Korbin in her kitchen consuming everything in sight—with no apparent regard for whether the tastes complimented so long as it was edible.

They were so preoccupied they didn't, in fact, seem to notice her at first.

It dawned on her, finally, what she was seeing.

Starvation.

The effects of it, at any rate.

Not one had said a word to her or let on that they were

weak from hunger—and thirst, too, if the way they were gulping down water was any indication.

A mixture of fury and pity and revulsion filled her.

They hadn't been given anything? Nothing? How could they do that to them? Pen them up to die and not even give them food and water?

This went beyond cruelty! *They* were the damned monsters! Not the cyborgs—who had been created to serve and had—with complete loyalty.

They were biological robots—primarily—and that meant they used the same fuel humans did, damn it! They *needed* it to operate!

And they needed water.

And they got weak with hunger, she realized as a memory surfaced of Raathe's grim determination to carry her through the sewers and not allow the others to touch her, but pausing briefly several times to adjust something, or stopping to 'get his bearings'.

He hadn't wanted to admit she was a burden to him.

That was just so ... illogical it sent another wave of uneasiness through her.

She dismissed it.

They were functioning outside the norm—learning to cope with a situation they hadn't been designed for.

Poor Caleb must be having the worst sort of time. He was a pleasure droid. He hadn't been designed for anything outside the brothel. There was absolutely no doubt in her mind that he'd been endowed with everything regarding sexuality that was known to man or science, but he had no function outside that and they hadn't wasted the storage space for data he wouldn't use anyway.

Raathe and Korbin had at least been programmed to handle military type situations.

They must have read her feelings in her expression because they glanced at her and stopped abruptly. She shook her head. "No! I'm sorry I interrupted. Go ahead

and have whatever you like. There's a processor over in
the corner. If you don't see anything you want you can
order it up and it'll be delivered. Or if you do see
something you want but there isn't enough."

"What will you eat?" Raathe asked.

She shook her head. "I'm so tired I can't think about
food right now. I'm just going to get a bath and then I'll
see if I feel like eating."

"I should check your foot to see what has happened
there," Korbin said.

She nodded. "But after the bath, ok?"

* * * *

Raathe was spoiling for a fight when he followed
Tabitha to the bathroom. Unfortunately for his successful
pursuit, the moment he saw her he completely forgot what
he had followed her in to argue about.

Tabitha had just rinsed her mouth and leaned down to
spit into the lavatory sink when she heard the bathroom
door open. She straightened abruptly and met Raathe's
gaze in the mirror over the lavatory.

A couple of seconds ticked off while he flicked a look
down her towel clad form and then he met her gaze again.
Fully expecting her to reject him in no uncertain terms,
possibly with violence, he said the first thing that came to
mind. "I thought it best to conserve time and resources by
sharing a bath."

Shock jolted through Tabitha and something else that
wasn't entirely unexpected, but certainly wasn't welcome
given the circumstances.

She felt her face heat with discomfort as memories
flooded back—of those awkward coming of age years
when she'd focused on Raathe, she supposed, because he
was really the only 'available' male she was around long
enough to practice flirtation.

She'd thought she had, long ago, broken herself of her
'crush' on Raathe.

Or at least that the humiliation of rejection had totally killed her interest in that direction.

That was what had inspired the visit to the brothel, anyway, and Caleb had certainly done his utmost to redirect her mind.

"You object to bathing with a machine?" he growled.

It occurred to Tabitha forcefully that it was a challenge issued, that he had intended the question to be provoking. Clearly, he was itching for a fight for some reason that escaped her. "No. It might be a little crowded …."

He ignored that caveat, stripping down before she could finish the sentence.

That was why she couldn't actually finish. She completely lost her train of thought when he peeled the top of his uniform off, revealing the broad, muscular chest and bulging arms she'd so often fantasized about when she was younger.

There was a light patch of hair between his male breasts that surprised her, occupied her mind until he unfastened his trousers and dropped them.

That was when she sucked in a sharp gasp and lost her grip on her towel.

She might have whipped around and put her back to him if she'd had possession of any of her faculties, but she didn't. Instead, mesmerized by the lance projecting from his belly, she followed it with her gaze until he turned and cut off her view.

He took his place at one end of the shower and waited for her.

She stared at him, knowing this was a very bad idea but completely unable to vocalize her doubts or think of a good excuse to leave.

He was waiting for her to turn the water on.

Jugged in the ass by that realization, she lurched forward and stepped clumsily inside.

He caught her shoulders, steadying her and then took a

scrub, lifted it toward a water outlet, and ordered the computer to soak them down with water at a temperature of one hundred five degrees.

Tabitha jerked as the water jetted out from every direction.

Raathe took one of her hands and placed her palm against the wall. "Brace here."

Tabitha didn't question the order. She lifted her other palm and placed it near the first to brace herself, but it was her knees that nearly buckled when Raathe ran the scrubber down her back from her shoulder to the crevice of her ass. A shudder ran through her.

"The water temperature is not satisfactory?"

Tabitha tried to speak and then cleared her throat and tried again. "I usually have it around one hundred ten— one fifteen if I'm chilled—but this is fine."

"The temperature makes no difference to me. I am a machine. I am only affected by temperature extremes. Computer—change the temperature to one hundred ten."

Tabitha didn't absorb the half of what he said. She was completely focused on the faintly rough texture of the scrub as he stroked her back with it—up to the shoulder, down to her buttocks, and then up again. She didn't even know when he set the scrub aside and began to use his palms to stroke and knead her back and buttocks, but she was floating very quickly on a sea of euphoria and it was all she could do to keep her knees locked.

"Rinse," he said as he picked up the scrub again and caught her arm. Guiding her away from the wall to stand in front of him, he crouched and began to scrub her front as he had her back—except he discarded the scrub fairly quickly in favor of rubbing the soap over her with his hands and then massaging her breasts and belly before he stroked two fingers along her cleft.

His expression was taut when he straightened, hard and unyielding.

Tabitha stared at him dizzily, feeling as detached from her body as if she was nothing more than a puppet for him to control.

Except that she felt weak and almost fevered.

He settled his hands on her waist after a moment, almost seemed to hesitate, and then he lifted her straight up.

She caught his shoulders instinctively for balance.

The hesitation that time was infinitesimal. Almost in one motion, he slipped his hands from her waist to her upper thighs, lifting her legs to his waist as he pressed her to the wall behind her and covered her mouth in a kiss of such savage need that it stole her breath from her chest. His mouth was as hard and unyielding as everything else about him—and it delighted her senseless. She felt his struggle for restraint, but it seemed a losing battle and that thrilled her even more.

He was shaking all over when he broke from her lips and sucked on the flesh beneath her ear.

"Tabby," he murmured raggedly.

The word was barely more than a breath of sound, and yet it raised goose bumps all over her body as his warm breath caressed her ear. It set her heart to hammering so hard it deafened her, made her feel faint and yet buoyant—almost like heated liquid.

He lifted her as he found her mouth again, this time tracing her cleft with something that seemed significantly larger than his finger. Visions of his fully erect cock flickered through her mind a moment before he found her opening and plugged it with the rounded head.

That divided her mind, shifting her focus from the intoxicating dance of his tongue along hers to his efforts to sheathe himself within her body and then back again—a seesaw reflection of his actions that made her feel as desperate to achieve a full joining as he seemed.

Fortunately, her want was liquid. It eased his passage, relieved the burn of flesh stretched almost beyond capacity as he delved deeper and deeper, inch by agonizing inch, until he had claimed every tiny patch of skin within her channel.

Raathe struggled to catch his breath and regain control as he felt his flesh fully engulfed by hers, felt the deep connection he had struggled so hard to achieve.

A sharp pain stabbed through his brain even as he managed total penetration, though, causing him to teeter for moments between complete failure of his mission and a complete loss of his hard fought control.

The pain clawed at his mind—almost like a memory trying to break into the open.

And yet, there could be no memory.

He had never touched Tabitha in such a way—not even close.

He had not dared even to want—not consciously.

Had it hovered on the fringes of consciousness?

And if so, how long?

Long enough to drive him mad with an itch he dared not scratch?

Since she had tortured him with desperate want so many years ago?

He did not know. It made no sense to him when he was as certain as he could be that total awareness was new to him, but it destroyed his attempts to maintain control, to regain control when it began to crumble.

He began to move abruptly, jerkily, with the burning desire consuming him alive. He found himself racing toward completion when the last thing on Earth he wanted was for this to end.

Tabitha found herself teetering on the brink of orgasm almost the second he began to move rhythmically inside of her. Each stroke of his flesh against hers set off fresh tremors until she was kissing him back as feverishly as he was kissing her, stroking his flesh everywhere that she could reach with her hands in an effort to flood her senses with him.

He came, so explosively that it set off a counter explosion inside of her. She gasped until she was virtually sobbing for breath, clinging tightly to him as the convulsions rocked her.

For long moments after the final quakes had faded away, they remained locked tightly together—almost as if Raathe was as reluctant to pull his flesh from her as she was to lose it.

Finally, he eased away from her, allowed her to slide gently to her feet.

When she had steadied herself, he turned away, picked up the scrub.

There was a faint tremor in his hand when he did so, but Tabitha barely noted it.

She was too busy struggling with her confusion.

What the hell had just happened, she wondered?

She felt perfectly blank—couldn't seem to string two thoughts together.

When the water came on again, she rinsed and stepped out, glancing back at Raathe, who had planted his palms against the far wall and leaned in to the water spraying from the jets.

Feeling a tickle on her inner thigh, she looked down and then simply stared in disbelief at the trail of semen snaking down her inner thigh.

Raathe was watching her when she looked up, his eyes narrowed on that snake trail. He met her gaze for a long moment. "Hard to comprehend, is it not, when you have never thought of me as anything more than a ... tool? A machine."

Those comments seemed to blast a path through to her consciousness. She blinked at him a couple of times. "I never thought of you as just a machine," she murmured. Turning, she crossed the bathroom to collect her towel and the change of clothing she'd gotten from her room.

Raathe's voice stopped her before she could leave. "This why you had no problem fucking the pleasure droid?" he growled.

Tabitha whipped around to stare at him, feeling a shockwave roll over her. The accusation spawned a mixture of angry resentment and guilt, but what quickly overshadowed both was the realization that the question indicated both jealousy and possessiveness—neither of which were things any cyborg should have felt.

Chapter Four

Apparently Korbin had been waiting for her to come out. As soon as she left the room, he shoved whatever it was he'd been eating into his mouth, dusted his hands and approached her. He pointed to her couch. "Sit there."

Tabitha wasn't actually in the mood to get her foot checked. Granted, it still hurt like hell, but she thought she was going to have to live with it until it stopped hurting. Moreover, Raathe had given her a lot of food for thought and all she really wanted to do at the moment was find some place to lick her wounds and figure out what had just happened.

She didn't want to go another round with him until she'd had the chance to compose herself and decide how to handle it—which was why she'd left her bedroom headed for her spare bedroom.

"I haven't had a chance to get dressed," she complained, flapping the clothes she'd collected from her room at him.

"That is good," he said. "I can examine you for other injuries."

Tabitha blinked at him, prompted by the comment to perform an internal evaluation. Truthfully, she felt like hell now that she'd had time to get over a lot of the shock of the battle she'd taken part in. She realized she was bruised and sore from it, but she couldn't honestly say that it was from the counterassault. Certainly a good bit of it would be nothing more than strained muscles from unaccustomed exercise. And she didn't detect anything that suggested a serious injury. She sat, though, deciding she might as well get it over with.

Korbin crouched immediately, reached to hook one hand behind her knee, and lifted her injured foot gently from the floor as he slipped his hand down her calf to her heel.

He studied it from every angle.

Every angle.

Even lifting her leg high so that he could look at her heel—supposedly.

His gaze flickered toward her crotch area several times, though, and she had the feeling the towel wasn't doing a great job of covering her privates.

But it actually sort of freaked her out a little to remind herself that he was a cyborg—not a perverted med tech—not a man at all—and then she didn't know how to react or even if she *should* react.

Wasn't *she* going to look like the nut job for pitching a fit about a cyborg studying her coochie?

Straightforward! "Are you looking at my … uh … genitals?" she demanded.

She didn't know whether to be charmed or terrified when he blushed.

And then … he *lied*.

He met her gaze for a long, long moment. "I thought that I detected some bruising. I believe it was only a shadow. If you will lift the towel I will examine it more carefully."

She stared at him doubtfully, trying to remember if she'd gotten hit anywhere near that area.

It was a waste of time, she discovered.

She'd been too wrapped up in the battle to notice anything beyond trying to hold the bastard off the button. Short of knocking her unconscious, she was pretty sure she wouldn't have really noticed where he hit her.

"You will need to remove the towel and lie down on the couch for me to finish the examination anyway."

She hesitated, but she really had no valid reason to refuse, she decided.

He was a med tech.

It would be stupid not to let him to examine her when she'd been in a fight.

Besides, he was a cyborg.

He wasn't going to hurt her.

His hands were so light, so gentle, it was almost more like being caressed than examined as he stroked them slowly over her breasts and belly.

Actually, it was a *lot* more like being caressed than examined.

Her eyes popped open and she found herself staring up at Raathe.

And he looked like the personification of wrath!

He was stark naked since he hadn't dressed or stopped to grab a towel.

His dragon had expired from their flight of fancy, but it still looked damned impressive at eye level.

She jackknifed upright so fast she almost butted heads

with Korbin. "Well? Everything check out ok?" she asked in a jittery voice.

Korbin frowned and then glared at Raathe, straightening to his full height and bracing himself as if he expected to come to blows with Raathe.

And he might well do so given the expression on Raathe's face.

Tabitha hopped up between them. "I'm going to go get dressed, guys!" she said with forced cheer, slipping between them to grab up the clothing she'd chosen.

Korbin's voice followed her to the door of the spare bedroom. "The foot is sprained. You will need to stay off of it as much as possible. I will wrap it with a pressure bandage once you have dressed."

"What the fuck was that all about?" Raathe asked in a low, threatening growl.

Korbin studied him thoughtfully for several moments. "I examined her—as I had said I would."

Raathe narrowed his eyes. "She did not injure her breasts," he ground out.

"No? I thought they looked bruised, but upon closer examination they appeared to be … abraded. Something like … whisker burn? In any case, she was in a fight with that bastard. She could have had injuries besides the most obvious."

Tabitha eased away from the door when she decided they weren't going to come to blows.

"Hello beautiful," Caleb murmured from the depths of the bed. "You can have no notion how much I have missed my baby."

Tabitha whipped around and stared at Caleb in shocked disbelief. "How did you …?"

"I came in here to bathe since you and Raathe were in the other bathroom and I thought that might be too crowded." He turned onto his side, propped his head on one hand, and patted the bed in invitation.

Tabitha smiled with an effort. "That is so ... unbelievably appealing! But I ...."

He lifted one dark brow questioningly. "But?"

She smiled with an effort, wondering now if she could slip out the corridor door from the bath as she'd planned and make it past Raathe and Korbin since they seemed to still be arguing if the voices she could hear dimly were anything to go by.

Because it had occurred to her as they made their way to her apartment that the door of opportunity was closing. Her father would not be gone long and then she wouldn't be able to access his files and she might never discover what was really going on, what was actually behind the recall and destruction of the cyborgs.

Then, too, there was the riot to consider. The protestors had broken in before they got out of the building and seemed bent on destroying as much as possible. She needed to try to slip in after they'd satisfied their rage and left and before the cops could move in to investigate. And before her father got back.

All in all, *now* seemed the best time to make her move—especially when the cyborgs all seemed preoccupied with rest and recovery to regain their strength.

And Raathe was preoccupied with Korbin at the moment and probably wouldn't notice that she'd slipped out until she had time to gain a fairly good lead.

She could use the path through the spare room and bath, out the guest door that led into the hall and then through the emergency exit—grab a cab and head back to the office ....

"Unless you would prefer to make love in the shower?"

That brought a swamping of memories that she wasn't ready to deal with at the moment. "Uh .... Why don't you just wait here while I ... uh ... well, I have something I need to take care of first."

Thankfully, he accepted the excuse and settled back against the pillows. "I will be waiting, baby."

Tabitha had barely cleared the door before she dove into the panties and tunic she'd selected in her room. She left the trousers dangling over her arm and carried the slippers she'd grabbed as she very carefully eased the other door to the bathroom open and peered down the hall toward the living area.

She could still hear a low voiced conversation between Raathe and Korbin, but she couldn't make out what they were saying or see either one.

She heard the door to the bedroom open abruptly, however, and then Raathe's voice. "What the fuck?"

Uh oh!

Stepping out of the bathroom, she hobbled toward the kitchen as fast as she could, trying to ignore the escalating sounds of fury and violence coming from her spare bedroom, and went out the door that led to the emergency exit. She paused once outside the apartment, while she was waiting for the elevator to arrive, and pulled her trousers on and then slipped her feet into the shoes.

Her injured foot was so swollen it was all she could do to get the shoe on that foot and she couldn't walk once she'd managed it.

She took the shoe off again as the elevator arrived and stepped inside the cabin.

She didn't breathe a sigh of relief, though, until the doors closed and the elevator began to drop toward the lobby.

An alarm Tabitha had never heard before went off just before the elevator cubicle stopped at the lobby level.

There were two cops standing at the elevator when the doors opened.

"That's her!" Frank the security guard exclaimed. "Ms. Langston."

"Oh shit! What?" Tabitha gasped, unable to focus on the disaster before her because her mind was on the potential catastrophe she'd left.

Raathe and Caleb were preoccupied with their fight and she had no way to warn them!

* * * *

Raathe was so pissed off at Korbin—certain despite his denials that he had taken advantage of the situation to grope Tabitha—that it took a few minutes for it to sink in that Tabitha had been gone longer than seemed reasonable.

A quick look told him Caleb was also nowhere in sight.

The instant that congealed in his mind, he broke off the heated discussion with Korbin and headed into the bedroom.

Caleb, he discovered, was propped up in the bed wearing nothing more than an expression of anticipation, clearly waiting for Tabitha. Whipping a quick look around and discovering she was not in the room did nothing to calm Raathe. He uttered a challenging bellow and leapt from the door to the middle of the bed, death in his eyes.

Fortunately for Caleb—who hadn't actually been given fight programming of any description—he was still able to recall his last encounter with Raathe with absolute clarity, in every detail—and he did have AI.

He whipped the cover off and rolled from the bed, sprawling on the floor beside it just as Raathe touched down in the middle of the bed—where he had been lying a split second before. He managed to push himself almost halfway up before Raathe waded across the mattress and planted a kick mid-belly that was hard enough to lift him from the floor and knock the breath from him. He tumbled sideways.

He did not manage to get up before Raathe leapt from the bed, but he did manage to grab Raathe's foot the next time he launched a kick.

Caught off guard, Raathe lost his balance and crashed into the floor hard enough to crack it—the floor—not any part of Raathe.

Caleb followed by leaping onto Raathe's chest and

curling his hands around Raathe's neck.

It was at just that moment that the two cops who'd headed up to knock on Tabitha's door decided the noise was definitely coming from inside her apartment and burst in.

Fortunately for Raathe and Caleb, the cops were so appalled at discovering two completely naked men rolling around on the floor that they were able to leap to their feet and charge through the bathroom—side by side—taking out the door and the wall on either side.

Korbin had already discovered the emergency exit through the kitchen—*before* the cops burst in. He had anticipated the arrival of the cops as soon as Caleb and Raathe began to take the apartment apart. His search for Tabitha had turned up nothing since she had already left, but since he knew she had not gone out the front that only left the possibility of a window—not likely—or an alternate exit.

He managed to get through it and into the corridor before either Raathe or Caleb caught up and moments before in dawned on the cops that they were dealing with a group of cyborgs and they began to spray the apartment down with their automatics.

Unwilling to wait for the cubicle to arrive, Korbin charged past the elevator and broke down the door to the stairs—which had been locked for security purposes—and made his way quickly down to ground level by leaping from one landing to the next.

Caleb followed so closely on his heels he nearly landed on him several times until Korbin had the forethought to knock him down. Raathe had stayed behind to slow the cops down by slamming the door into them and knocking both men out, but still caught up and followed closely enough to shove Caleb out of the way before he could leap again.

In spite of their race to be first to jump, or maybe due to

it, the three managed to arrive at the lobby just in time to see the two cops that had waylaid Tabitha escorting her from the building to the patrol car waiting outside.

Raathe was ready to charge across the lobby and stop them, but Korbin blocked his path. "They have not arrested her."

Raathe paused, struggling with the sense of urgency he always felt to protect Tabby at all costs. "How do you know?" he growled.

"Because she is not in handcuffs. They will let her go. We just have to find a place where we can watch and get her back when they release her."

Raathe did not like the idea. He would have felt better to retrieve her immediately and nursed the fear that it would only become harder to get her back the longer they waited.

But when he saw that Korbin had delayed him until the cops had gotten into the car and left, he decided that they might as well wait a little while and see if Korbin was right.

If he was wrong then he could always beat the fuck out of the bastard after they got Tabitha back.

* * * *

"When was the last time you saw your father?" the elder of the two detectives—Joe Barnes—asked.

Tabitha blinked at him, struggling to make sense of the question in connection with them picking her up to interrogate her. It was no use. Nothing that had happened that day had made any damned sense and this was just another episode of crazy.

She could've understood if they'd launched an interrogation about the incident in her father's factory. She had actually *expected* that. Whether or not the floor manager had survived, he'd certainly been assaulted—by her and then Raathe—so that was criminal and connected to her and she thought there might actually have been some cameras that could have caught the crime or at least them entering and then leaving around the time it happened. It would have terrified her if they'd launched into that, but it would've made sense for them to take her into custody and take her to the police station and park her in an interrogation room with two older but tough looking detectives.

Dragging her down to the station and then asking her about her father?

Had they done any kind of background investigating—at all?

She didn't even *live* with her father anymore—actually hadn't lived with him a hell of a lot when she was growing up, but now she didn't even live at his estate anymore. She had her own apartment in town.

And yes, he was her boss, technically speaking because he ran the company where she worked, but he wasn't her supervisor.

And she'd certainly never been allowed to keep up with his comings and goings as employee or daughter.

"Uuuh," she said, stalling for time since she certainly didn't want to incriminate herself in anything in any possible way if she could help it. "What's this about?"

"Just answer the question, please," Detective Will Johnson said sternly.

He was playing bad cop, she decided. "I don't think so," she responded coolly, "not unless you want to let me know what this is about."

"Do you have anything to hide?"

That was bad cop. Tabitha stared at the man in outrage.

"Because it seems to me that you must or you would be cooperating."

Ok so they were playing bad cop worse cop not bad cop good cop.

"Cooperating with what?" she demanded finally.

"Our investigation."

"What damned investigation? You haven't told me a

damned thing!"

"We asked you to answer some questions," bad cop one said tightly. "You agreed to come with us and answer them and now you refuse to cooperate."

Tabitha studied the man for a long moment. "I did answer," she said after a moment.

"No. You asked what the question was about."

"And *you* didn't answer it!" she said with an ah ha attitude.

"Because we aren't here to answer your questions," bad cop one growled.

"Well! I don't see why not! You're the one that isn't cooperating. I was perfectly civil! And if you aren't going to arrest me for something you've cooked up, then I think I'll leave because I don't like your attitude!"

"When was the last time you spoke to your father?" bad cop two demanded when she started to get up.

Tabitha considered the question. She didn't see any way that it could incriminate her at all, but could it incriminate her father?

And did she care?

She thought she didn't, but she always thought that when she was angry with him and, deep down, she didn't actually want harm to come to him.

Still—she thought she could answer this one with complete honesty. "I think …. Well, I'm not entirely sure, but it seems to me that I talked to him last week."

Both cops stared at her as if she had two heads.

"Let me get this straight—you work with father? But you haven't spoken to him for a week?"

"Well, I don't actually work *with* my father. He's CEO of the company and I'm in the research and development department."

"But you do work for him?"

Tabitha shrugged. "Technically, I suppose. But in reality, I work for the board that owns the company. He just handles the Southern Division."

Both men stared at her with a mixture of anger and disbelief. "I don't think I understand why it is that talking with you is like pulling teeth, Ms. Langston."

"Oh! Now you're going to accuse me of not cooperating again *just* because you don't like the answer? Well! I can't tell you how much it grieves me that you don't, but it's the truth!"

"So—you're saying that you haven't seen or spoken to your father in …." He stopped and looked at his notes. "Somewhere in the neighborhood of a week and you have no idea where he might be?"

Tabitha gave the man a look. "I didn't say that."

"What do you mean you didn't say that?"

"I didn't say I had no idea where he was."

She got the distinct impression they were thinking about throttling her—something about the way they were looking at her.

"So you do know where your father is?"

"Well—I know where he said he was going. Pretty much everybody in upper management got the memo, I'm sure."

"And?"

"What?"

"The memo?"

"Oh! He was supposed to be leaving town yesterday evening for a meeting at headquarters."

"Would it shock you to know that that, in fact, is not where he is?"

Tabitha gaped at him for a moment before indignation filled her. "Well! If you knew he wasn't there why the hell have you been browbeating me to tell you? I don't know where he'd be if he isn't where he said he was going!"

"You're certain you have no knowledge of his whereabouts?"

Uneasiness replaced Tabitha's anger. "Why are you

looking for my father? Exactly what is it that you think he's done?"

"We think he might have gotten himself kidnapped and murdered, Ms. Langston. That's why we brought you in— to see if you had any information that might help us find him. He never made it to the spaceport. We found his bullet ridden car about six miles from the port."

Tabitha stared at him, feeling every word like a bullet slamming into her. It was just too much—way too much after everything else. She abruptly felt very heavy and darkness began to invade her vision. "I don't …. You're saying …."

"That he's missing and there is a strong indication that he may be dead."

The last thing Tabitha remembered was trying to brace herself on the desk in front of her to keep from slipping to the floor. But then she heard chairs scraping the floor, muffled voices and she felt herself drifting down and the gritty, cold floor against her cheek for a handful of moments before darkness engulfed her.

Chapter Five

"You two are not necessary. I will wait for Tabitha. You may take yourselves off," Raathe said. He was not particularly hopeful that he could convince them to go away at this point, but he thought it worth a try since it also seemed unlikely that he would be able to shake them.

Actually, if the circumstances had been different, he would not have been especially perturbed about their determination to stick with him—that circumstance being Tabitha.

She was far too trusting, though, and willing to bestow her affection indiscriminately because she had never gotten the affection she had so desperately wanted. She believed that giving would bring affection back to her and that was, unfortunately, not something that could be counted upon.

At all.

Because those willing and capable of giving affection would offer it just as she did—with generosity and without expectation of receiving.

And Caleb and Korbin, he felt certain, were hanging after her because both understood that about her—either consciously or unconsciously—that she was vulnerable and an easy mark.

He did not suppose he would have worried overmuch about that, truth be told, except he had begun to suspect that all was not right with him and he could not entirely dismiss the fear that he might fail Tabby—leaving her vulnerable to predators.

The sharp, stabbing pains in his head that he had been experiencing since he had attained awareness were becoming more frequent and debilitating. He had no idea what was causing it, no way of finding out, or any way to determine whether it would result in catastrophic failure at some point.

He thought if that happened that Tabitha would be safer

with her own kind—with humans—or more specifically her father.

He was a total bastard, but he had always seen to it that Tabitha was protected.

Raathe knew she would be safe with him.

He was not convinced that she would be safe with Caleb and Korbin because, aside from the fact that it was clear to him that both of them were champing at the bit to climb between her thighs, neither one was fully prepared or programmed for such a complex task. Caleb could fuck like a champion and Korbin could fight like one, but neither of them had a full enough understanding of humans to protect Tabitha from them. And both of them were being hunted.

Caleb and Korbin both turned to stare at Raathe in gathering outrage.

"I will not leave her," Korbin said flatly. "I am her man."

"Where the fuck did you get that idea?" Raathe growled challengingly. "*I* am her man! I have been her man since I was created. It is *my* duty to protect her from all threats and it always has been."

"She risked her life to save mine," Korbin growled back. "I owe her my loyalty and my protection! And I will not leave because you say so! If *she* sends me away, then I will go."

"She did not risk her life to save you! She risked her life to save me," Caleb said indignantly. "It was I who called to her and she responded by setting me free! *I* am her lover."

Raathe punched him in the face. "She fucked you. That is all! That does not make her your lover or vice versa!"

"What would you know about it? You are not a pleasure model!"

Raathe grabbed him by the throat.

Caleb reciprocated, tightening his hands on Raathe's

throat.

"If you two begin to fight and draw the cops, I will have nothing to do with it," Korbin said tightly.

Raathe glared at Caleb several moments more and then released him and knocked Caleb's hands from his throat. "He is right. I cannot risk being taken in by the cops. I will beat the fuck out of you later."

"I think now would be a good time to find clothing," Korbin said pointedly.

"And leave you to take off with Tabby when she is released?" Raathe growled. "I do not think so."

Korbin shrugged. "It will attract attention we do not want if you two stroll outside like that."

"No one can see us here in the sewers," Raathe said pointedly. "That is something that can wait."

Unfortunately, they did not see Tabitha leave as they had expected. Instead, after what seemed an unreasonable length of time to Raathe, an ambulance arrived. Uneasiness flickered through him when two med techs dove out, grabbed a gurney from the back, and rushed inside. Perhaps thirty minutes passed and they headed out again. This time, though, there was someone strapped to the stretcher.

Tabitha shoved the oxygen mask off. "I told you I was fine! I just fainted, that's all!"

Consternation filled the hearts of the three waiting in the sewer and watching through the storm drain.

"I *knew* you were more focused on feeling her up than checking to see if she was ok," Raathe growled, grabbing Korbin by the throat.

"I believe I will go to the hospital to discover what is wrong with my baby. You two may stay and be arrested if you like," Caleb said, turning away and trotting briskly through the sewer pipe.

Korbin and Raathe broke off grappling with one another. Raathe leapt away, focused on catching up to Caleb.

Korbin managed to trip Raathe up before he could get hold of Caleb and then shouldered Caleb out of the way as he passed him. They still managed to arrive at the medical center in a dead heat, but not in time to prevent the techs from taking Tabitha inside.

Not that that had been the plan any of the time.

Raathe wanted her properly looked at and cared for. He needed to know that nothing was seriously wrong with her and when she would be in a condition to be safely moved. And it was obvious to him now that he could not depend upon Korbin for that. That stupid bastard could not focus beyond touching her.

Granted, he had had some difficulty focusing on anything else, but Korbin was a med tech, damn it!

Obviously, the longer they lingered the more danger for all of them.

But he was more concerned about Tabby.

He could take whatever they threw at him if he had to—up to and including the furnace.

He could not take anything happening to Tabby.

He would not allow it.

But the only way to prevent it was to make certain the authorities did not manage to lock her away and charge her for the incident back at the company—any part of it.

Even if it meant that he would have to turn her over to her father to protect her, he meant to do it.

He did not relish that thought.

He was of the opinion that her father had never been good to her. In fact, he was cruel quite often even though he had never, to Raathe's knowledge, actually harmed her physically.

But he was a powerful man—a powerful human with great wealth and that was all that Raathe knew of that might save Tabby from her misguided efforts to save him.

And, whatever Caleb or Korbin said to the contrary, he knew that she had risked everything for *him*. She had never seemed to understand completely or care that he was nothing but a machine. He knew she had felt fondness because she had always tried to protect him from her father.

Or course, he was generally in danger from her father because he had failed in some manner to protect her as expected—because she had a knack for running off and getting herself into trouble. But that did not change the fact that she would not allow her father to punish him for what she had done in spite of every effort on his part to prevent her from doing whatever it was she had gotten into trouble for.

* * * *

Tabitha was not happy about the ambulance ride from the police station. She'd always hated attracting attention—particularly any negative sort of attention. But then again, she supposed she couldn't be entirely dissatisfied about it since it had very effectively terminated the interrogation.

She was still inclined to be weepy about that horror story they'd sprung on her that had brought on the faint.

But, in her heart of hearts, did she believe it?

She didn't know.

Her father was wily—and borderline paranoid. It seemed completely out of character for him to be caught off guard and ambushed like that.

Unfortunately, that was no guarantee that he hadn't been. Something horrible had happened, for sure, to convince the cops that he'd been dragged off and then murdered. And, apparently, she was their number one suspect.

She was damned if she knew why.

She hated her father as often as she felt any affection for him—maybe more often—but nobody knew that! She didn't go around telling people she hated him.

Because, truthfully, she really didn't have anyone close that she could confide in.

A good bit of that was entirely her father's fault, too, because he had made it impossible for her to form any early bonds with other children. She'd reached adulthood with nothing more than shadow bonds—no close or tight family bonds, and nothing outside that really counted beyond friendly acquaintance.

And she hadn't been able to change that as a young adult.

In point of fact, she was very quickly becoming as big a recluse as her father—not because she wanted that for herself but because her upbringing, and maybe her genes, had made her different and she just couldn't fit in no matter how hard she tried. She couldn't find anyone that she had enough in common with to click.

God knew she'd tried! She'd dated obsessively for a while when she finally shook her father loose and had the chance.

She'd gotten tired of the parade of men interested in her father very quickly, though. Because it seemed to her that that was what they found most attractive about her—daddy's wallet—even men from families at least as wealthy as hers.

Maybe mostly them.

The long, long wait in the emergency room gave her some time to collect herself and try to fit puzzle pieces together to try to understand what had happened or might have.

She couldn't think of anything in the memo about the trip that suggested her father had other plans. In point of fact, the collection for the recall had already begun so it seemed doubtful her father had made that up.

Well, she supposed he might have, come to think on it.

Wouldn't it be more likely that that meeting would have taken place before the recall started?

Unless, of course, it was about the preliminary discoveries they'd made investigating the claims against the company?

Ok so possible and really that made a lot of sense. He was on the board. Money was god and nothing more important so a meeting to discuss how they could cut their losses ....

But he hadn't made it to the airport/spaceport.

So had he been set up?

Or had someone known or discovered he was going out of town and seized the opportunity?

But why? Who? And, assuming her father had gotten away, where had he gone?

And if he hadn't gotten away and was still alive, she thought in sudden horror?

That thought brought her off the examination table.

She almost slammed into the doctor coming in as she was heading out.

He looked around in confusion. "Are you the patient they brought in?"

Tabitha shook her head. "I can't sit around here all night waiting to be looked at. Sorry."

"You'll need to sign a waiver stating that you refused treatment!" he called after her.

She shot him a bird and kept walking as briskly as she could.

She'd more than half expected him to summon the guard to waylay her before she could get out without giving them some money, but she managed to make it to the exit without a challenge.

She emerged into night and the sounds of battle still raging.

She supposed it must not be too late if the riot was still in full swing. Surely to god they were going to get tired and go home after a while?

As she hesitated, trying to decide where to go, Korbin appeared near the corner of the building and headed straight for her.

She debated, briefly, whether to go with him or not—especially since it had occurred to her that they might be kidnapping her to barter their freedom—but she really had no one to turn to, she realized. They might not help her, but it wasn't as if she had someone she could call for help.

He stopped when he reached her, scanning her length. "You did not see a doctor," he said flatly. "You must go back and let them do tests so that we know you are not hurt."

That was so sweet and thoughtful Tabitha thought for several moments that she was going to burst into tears.

No one had ever worried that she might be hurt.

Not that she remembered, anyway. She supposed her mother might have, but no one since.

Except Raathe. He had guarded her like a hen with one chick, but she knew now that he had been programmed to and that took a lot of the power out of it. As a child it had made her feel like she at least had one person in the world that cared—because she'd thought of Raathe as a person. He'd seemed just as real as the other people around her—actually warmer and more human.

She cleared her throat. "I just fainted. I'm fine."

He frowned. "You are not fine if you fainted! There was something wrong or you would not have fainted."

"They're going to catch you if we stand here arguing."

"Then they will catch me," he said, taking her arm and turning her about. "I must know that you are alright."

"Really! It was just the shock of … well everything, I guess."

"And once I have seen that you have guessed right then I will feel comfortable to take you away from here."

There was something to be said for behaving as if one belonged. Korbin marched her right into the hospital and to an examination room. When she had stripped again and lain down, he moved a scanner into place and stepped over to the control console. He stood there, watching the data as it was presented, until she had been scanned from head to toe.

"Nothing detected beyond the sprained foot," he said, looking at her at last.

"See? I told you."

A faint smile curled his lips that made her belly do a jitter and warmth flush lower regions.

She realized she hadn't really looked at him in all the time he'd been with her. She'd been too distracted by Raathe and Caleb.

Like all cyborgs—particularly the soldier series—he was built like a god, of course, perfectly proportioned, perfect posture—and perfectly symmetrical facial features. But it went beyond that. Like Caleb, who'd been designed as a pleasure bot, his face was pretty boy handsome, pleasing enough to make her belly shimmy in appreciation.

"And yet I have gotten the impression from Raathe that you are devious and prone to lying," he responded.

Tabitha gaped at him. "I am ... not," she said, stumbling over the denial and then added with more truth. "That was when I was a kid! I had to then because of my father. I don't have to now. I'm free."

It was unfortunate that the comment reminded her that she might well be permanently free because it brought sadness down upon her with an abruptness that made her suddenly tearful. She sniffed. "I might not have to worry about that at all anymore. The cops said ...." She stopped, trying to regain control of her chin.

Korbin was either concerned she would have hysterics and draw unwanted attention or just unwilling to deal with it himself. "Tell me later," he said, quickly moving to the supply cabinet and rifling through it. He returned in a few moments with a pressure bandage and applied it to her foot.

The cessation of pain was almost instantaneous.

The relief nearly overwhelming.

"We have to go. Raathe and Caleb are waiting in the

sewers, but they are liable to grow impatient. And then we may have more trouble than we can sort through."

Just their bad luck, they ran into the same damn doctor that Tabitha had thoroughly pissed off as they headed out. He tried to stop them by blocking their path.

Korbin caught him by the throat, lifted him off the floor and then dropped him to one side.

Tabitha didn't think it would have attracted a lot of attention if not for that, but he made a lot of noise when he hit the floor and even as busy as the emergency room was that caught everyone's attention.

Fortunately, they were only a few strides from the exit and managed to get through it before the doctor began to bellow for help.

Korbin scooped Tabitha off her feet and jogged down the stairs with her and then around the side of the hospital while everyone gaped at them.

Raathe and Caleb, still stark naked, were standing by the culvert when they turned the corner, the pair having apparently just climbed out.

"Did you find clothing?" Caleb asked.

"I did not have time," Korbin responded.

Raathe was studying Tabitha, struggling with his resentment at seeing her in Korbin's arms. "She is alright?"

Korbin nodded. "I ran a scan. There was nothing detected beyond the sprain we already knew about."

Raathe frowned, unconvinced, but he dropped through the culvert opening behind Caleb.

Korbin lowered her into Raathe's waiting arms and then climbed down and closed the manhole cover.

"Why did they bring her here in an ambulance?" Raathe demanded. "This does not seem right."

Tabitha sighed. "I was upset with what they told me and … I just fainted."

Raathe's arms tightened around her, but as much as he

wanted to know what had upset her they could not simply stand around and chat, he knew. It did not appear that they had been seen entering the sewers, but he knew the cops would be arriving with dogs at any time and they needed to put as much distance between them and the medical center as possible.

Chapter Six

It was just as well the guys moved quickly. They had not gone very far before they heard sounds behind them indicating that the cops had arrived and decided to check the sewers.

Fortunately, it took them a little while to verify that their group had taken to the sewers and longer to put together a task force and get dogs down to help with the search. Not that the dogs would be much help when there was standing water in the sewers, but the collection system branched in every direction and the cops needed all the help they could get to avoid having to split their search group up.

Thankfully, it was shortly after hearing the first baying dogs that they reached a manhole Raathe determined was close to the outskirts of town and they all climbed out.

There was a taxi near the end of the block. After a brief debate, they decided to approach it and confiscate the vehicle for their use.

They were in luck—not so much the driver who'd dozed off at the wheel.

Raathe punched the window out and dragged the hapless man through it, knocking him out cold before Tabitha could even think to object.

She saw immediately why, however, since Raathe dropped the man to the ground and promptly pulled the man's pants off and stepped into them.

It was obvious immediately that the man was a good bit shorter than Raathe and much rounder. The pants legs fit like capris and the waistband didn't fit at all. Even fastened and belted the pants slipped down his hips and he had to keep hitching them up again to preserve his modesty.

Caleb—a day late and a dollar short—ended up with the man's shirt—and nothing else.

Tabitha didn't know which looked the most obscene— the overlarge trousers slipping down Raathe's hips and threatening to fall off or the shirt Caleb had tied around his waist—because the sleeves didn't actually cover a damn thing! In point of fact, they acted more like a frame for his bare genitals than cover.

"Well at least you covered your ass," she murmured.

Caleb looked down at himself and then back at her in confusion.

Obviously, he couldn't see anything looking down but the knot he'd tied.

She bit her lip and, on impulse, patted his cheek. "Never mind, sweety."

He looked disconcerted, but he smiled back.

Raathe glared disapprovingly at both of them. "Your cock is hanging out, you dim wit," he growled.

Caleb reddened and looked down again.

"That was mean, Raathe!" Tabitha said angrily, realizing

that the comment made it seem as if she'd been making fun of him.

Sure enough, she saw hurt and anger in Caleb's eyes when she glanced at him. Giving the shirt a twist that left the tie at one thigh, he stalked around the taxi and climbed in.

"Thanks a lot," she growled at Raathe and then climbed into the back seat beside Caleb as Raathe got into the driver's seat and Korbin took shotgun.

When everyone had settled and fastened belts, Raathe started the vehicle and took off, leaving the naked taxi driver laying in the street.

But not for long!

Clearly he'd been faking unconsciousness because the car hadn't even turned the corner before he popped up and took off running in the opposite direction.

Tabitha was relieved.

Not Korbin or Raathe.

"Shit! He will go straight to the nearest cop!" Raathe muttered, hesitating, clearly wondering if he should go back.

"Leave him," Korbin said. "The cops are already looking. They will not be far behind by now anyway."

"You should remove the tracking device," Caleb volunteered.

Both Korbin and Raathe whipped around to look at him in surprise.

"What? You think I know nothing? As it happens I made several attempts to escape and I know this from experience."

Tabitha whipped a shocked, questioning look in his direction.

"Well a couple," Caleb amended. "Once not long after you came …. The last when I awakened."

"Did you remove your own tracker?" Korbin asked sharply.

Caleb gave him an indignant look. "Yes. That is why I know it was the taxi they were tracking."

Raathe pulled off of the road abruptly and into the open door of a derelict warehouse he had spotted. There were no lights inside, of course, but they did not actually need them to scan the vehicle for a tracking device.

That was when Raathe made a very unpleasant discovery.

Tabitha was fitted with a tracking device.

"Why did you say nothing about this?" he asked as they got back into the vehicle and he turned it around to head out once more, trying to keep his voice carefully neutral.

She looked at him wide eyed—that look she had so often given her father when she was a small child caught in a lie.

"I forgot about it! I swear it! I would've said something." It crushed her that he still looked unconvinced, that he could believe she would deceive him about something that could get him terminated. It also gave rise to another flicker of dread that their reasons for keeping her with them might not be benign at all.

"She is human," Caleb growled. "Their memory is not as reliable as ours and, if she was a child, then she has had much time to forget."

She hugged Caleb impulsively for defending her when he must know Raathe was looking for any excuse to pound on him.

Because he wanted him *away* from her, she realized.

She also realized that it was *her* fault.

In high school, she had decided that she was ready for sex. Everyone else was having sex. She didn't want to be a freak. More of a freak.

Besides, she was curious and her libido had awakened. She had urges. She desired. She had convinced her high school crush to sneak into her room one night for recreation, but Raathe had caught him before he had even managed to get in the window and had tossed him out again. After that, she couldn't even convince him to meet her anywhere else because he was terrified that Raathe would make good on his threat to rip him in half.

Then—her most painful and embarrassing memory—she'd tried to seduce Raathe.

He had informed her that he was a CHS300 and not programmed with human sexuality. He could not perform for her and he was a machine so he was unable to feel the passion she'd wanted or even to pretend that he did.

That was when she'd decided she was *going* to get laid—one way or another.

They weren't going to blight her life forever! Raathe and her father! She hadn't gotten to experience hardly any of the things most kids took for granted.

So she'd researched until she found the brothel, studied the available pleasure droids, and chosen Caleb.

And he had fulfilled her wildest dreams—for hours.

And then Raathe had found them.

She'd *wanted* Raathe to find them together, known he would report the incident directly to her father who probably wouldn't have believed her if she'd told him straight out.

But she'd also wanted to punish Raathe for refusing her and making her feel unwanted and unattractive, she realized.

Because she couldn't accept that Raathe felt nothing.

Deep down, she'd always believed he was secretly real.

She'd never been able to think up a reason for the impersonation of an android, but that hadn't killed the fantasy.

She supposed because if she accepted that he wasn't real then she also had to accept that the one person in the world that she thought cared about her didn't because he wasn't capable of it.

"It's not that I actually forgot," she told Raathe. "It's

just that I got used to it a long time ago and I don't really think about it. Haven't because ... well, there didn't seem any point in trying to run away anymore. Father always sent you after me and then he sent me away."

The comments made Raathe uncomfortable—for several reasons.

Primarily because he had known she had a tracking device when she was small. It was how he kept up with her.

But she was not a child anymore. Why would she still have it?

"We cannot remove it here," Korbin pointed out. "It is too deep. In any case, we need to move before the cops catch up to us."

"And we don't have to worry about Father tracking me. He's ... missing."

"This is what upset you?" Raathe asked sharply.

She nodded.

Caleb patted her arm. "We will find the old bastard. Do not worry."

Tabitha bit her lip, torn between sobbing and laughter. "Caleb! Why would you say that?"

His eyes widened. "What part?"

"Calling him an old bastard."

He frowned. "That is what you called him. I thought that that was his name."

Guilt swamped Tabitha. It took no more than a moment to recall that that was how she usually referred to him when she was a teen. And she'd been a teen when she'd gone to Caleb for sex.

Actually, she still thought of him more often than not as the old bastard.

Because he was a hateful man! He always had been. It wasn't just because he was old now.

But she was torn. He was missing. He could be in distress. The people that took him might be torturing him to get information.

He might already be dead.

She didn't have to struggle to figure out that she would be sad if it was true, that she *did* care about him in spite of everything.

Maybe she was a fool for loving him in spite of all he'd done, in spite of her certainty that he'd never loved her, but she did.

She didn't want him to be dead.

And that thought finally pierced her grief and shock with something helpful, something that gave her hope, made her feel as if she was on the verge of finding him. "Father has a tracking device, too. He had one put in each of us years and years ago in case anyone tried to kidnap us for ransom."

* * * *

There were cops waiting at the gates of the estate. Raathe slowed the vehicle.

"Do you think they're here for me?" Tabitha asked uneasily. "Or looking for Father?"

Raathe shook his head. "I do not know, but I do not believe it will be in our best interest to stop to chat with them."

"What now?" Korbin asked. "You and Caleb have lost your weapons. I have the rifle and some grenades from the security office, but I do not think it is enough to rout them."

Raathe flicked a sharp look at him. "I did not notice that you got them. How many?"

Korbin stared at him for a long moment, clearly summoning the information from memory. "I have three flash bangs, four smoke bombs and two teargas grenades."

"What is your throwing range?"

Again, Korbin simply stared while he mentally calculated. "One mile. But the timers will not allow for that distance. We must be within half a mile or they will go off before they reach the target."

"Good enough. There is a back entrance, but I have no desire to lead them there so that they know positively that we are inside. You must launch the grenades in rapid succession to confuse and blind them when we reach the launch point and then I will floor it and try to reach the hidden entrance before they can recover and give chase."

Tabitha turned and looked at Caleb uneasily and then searched the seat for safety belts and secured hers—just in case the plan didn't go off as described.

In actuality, it was damn close. Raathe 'floored' it as soon as he and Korbin had settled on their plan. Korbin put the window down and climbed halfway out, removing the pins from the grenades and holding three in each hand until they reached what he considered the launch point. As soon as he'd pitched them, he grabbed the rest, prepared them and launched them toward the cops as Raathe made the sudden turn.

Tabitha was amazed he didn't manage to sling Korbin out.

She thought Korbin must have been prepared for it, braced for it, but the glare he sent Raathe seemed to indicate he *still* wasn't happy about it.

The cops managed to get off a few rounds when they saw Raathe barreling down on them, but the smoke, teargas, and flash bangs effectively distracted, blinded and deafened them just before Raathe went into his turn and sped off—straight toward the mountain the estate backed up to.

Tabitha thought she might have been frightened if she hadn't been distracted by the fact that the car was about to beat her to death because Raathe was driving so fast over rough terrain that wasn't actually a road. It was all she could do to focus on staying in the seat with both the safety belt and Caleb to hold her down. Just before they reached the rocky outcropping, a wide mouth opened. Raathe slammed on the brakes as they crossed the threshold and skidded into a swearing halt that brought the vehicle around a hundred eighty degrees. Leaping from the car the moment he brought it to a jarring halt, he jogged to the control console adjacent to the door and sent the drones out to 'sweep' their tracks even as the doors closed.

The interior lights came on a few seconds behind the sealing of the mountain.

As shaken as she was from the close encounter with the cops and Raathe's wild evasive maneuvers, Tabitha unfastened her belt and clambered out on shaky legs, looking around in stunned amazement. "What is this place?"

Raathe whipped a sharp glance at her. "You did not know of it?"

Tabitha shook her head. "I guess … Father had it built?"

Raathe shrugged. "I do not know. He may have, but that was before my time. It was already part of the security when I came. This is why I have remote access codes to enter."

Tabitha nodded and began to look around. The area where Raathe had stopped the vehicle looked pretty much like an ordinary garage … except that the door looked like part of the mountain from the outside. After a moment, she followed the hallway that led off of it. The door at the end opened automatically as she neared it and lights began to flicker to life, flooding what she discovered was an opulent, and vast, cavern.

It was strongly reminiscent of an open, multi-level shopping mall in many regards. An elaborate, classical fountain took center stage and came on at their entrance. A sweeping, horseshoe staircase embraced it and led from the bottom floor to the upper level.

There the similarities ended.

The area around the fountain was tiled, but plush carpet, designed to look like area rugs, filled the remainder of the space. Furniture groupings occupied perhaps half of the 'area' rugs—comfortable overstuffed chairs, sofas, and tables.

There was a wall of TVs in the space beneath the upper landing. They came on as Tabitha approached, displaying views outside the estate walls.

The cops were no longer camped outside the main gate, she saw, but a good bit of smoke still lingered.

Another camera caught a view of their vehicle taillights as they raced past the opening to the mountain, heading toward the back gate of the estate.

Clearly they didn't have a warrant or they would already have stormed the gates.

Of course, they would have to scale them unless they'd brought explosives to blast through. Her father had had the place fortified.

There were other views from cameras set elsewhere— some from the office building in town showing that the riots were still in full swing even though it must be close to mid-night by now. Cameras covered all four aspects from the office towers and were mounted high enough she could see a couple of blocks away.

There was also one dedicated to the interior of the office that paused briefly for viewers to gaze down hallways and into offices—in a cascading effect—starting at the lobby and moving up the building floor by floor.

She left the monitors shortly after the men joined her to stare at first one and then another, on the hunt for a computer console. She found one set up in the middle of one of the 'conversation' groupings and settled with shaking hands to pull up the trackers.

The screen she pulled up stunned and confused her, though.

It showed her tracker exactly where she was sitting.

And her father's only a matter of yards away.

That couldn't be.

It just wasn't ….

"He's here!" she gasped, leaping to her feet and dashing down the hallway that led off the main living area.

There were four doors.

She stopped to check each.

"He is in his office," Raathe called after her. "It is the last door on the left."

She'd already checked all of the doors except that one, but she hardly registered the irritation about the timeliness of that information. She rushed to the door he'd indicated and flung it open. "Father?"

The room was as devoid of life as the other three she'd checked—a bathroom, a closet and the kitchen. Stunned, confused, she simply stood in the center of the room, making a slow sweep with her gaze as if it would have surprised her less to discover him in hiding.

Raathe and then, more slowly, Korbin and Caleb joined them.

They also stopped to search the room with their gazes.

Abruptly, Raathe took two long strides to reach the desk and picked up something.

"What is it?" Tabitha gasped.

Raathe was frowning when he met her gaze. "It is his tracker. He removed it."

Tabitha moved close enough to examine the tiny object herself and then abruptly burst into tears.

She didn't think she could have done anything else that would have cleared the room nearly as effectively.

Raathe and Korbin exchanged a stunned look of dismay and then both retreated toward the door.

Caleb hesitated and then moved toward her, slipping an arm around her shaking shoulders. "It is alright, baby. Cry if you need to."

At the invitation, Tabitha collapsed against his shoulder and sobbed louder.

Caleb simply stood where he was for a few moments

and then very carefully scooped her into his arms and turned toward the door with her.

Raathe and Korbin both gave him a wide berth but followed as he headed down the hallway with her, looked around, and then climbed the stairs. Opening the first door he came to, he examined the bedroom and decided it would do as well as any since it was furnished and lavishly appointed.

Raathe and Korbin stopped at the door.

Raathe frowned ferociously, but he didn't want to divert Tabitha's attention to him and Caleb just ignored him.

After watching while Caleb settled her carefully on the bed and then sat on the edge and gathered her onto his lap, he left—angry that Caleb had usurped him but feeling less than adequate for the task at hand.

He had never been able to handle Tabitha's tears—not even before the awakening when he should have been ruled completely by logic and totally immune to human emotions.

Korbin hesitated and then went out, as well, closing the door behind him.

He discovered that Raathe had crossed the main living area and gone out through a door on the other side. Curious, he followed and found that there was a fully equipped med bay about halfway down that corridor— found because that was where he discovered that Raathe had headed.

Raathe settled on the examination table and lay down.

Korbin moved to the control console. "What are we looking for?"

Raathe said nothing for a moment. "I believe that I may be dying. I need a scan of my brain to see if this issue can be verified or dismissed as non life threatening."

Chapter Seven

Tabitha wept until she had exhausted her supply of tears and began to sniff to contain the 'drip'. Caleb pulled off his shirt/skirt and handed it to her to dry her tears and blow her nose.

She supposed she should have refused it, particularly since that left him buck ass naked. She should have gotten up and gone in search of tissue, but she didn't really feel like moving.

She had been so certain that the tracker would lead her to her father!

And then convinced she would find him working in his office.

"Do you think my father is dead?" she asked forlornly.

Caleb patted her, considering his answer carefully. "I believe that we have found nothing to indicate that he is."

She lifted her head and shifted away from him to study his expression and decided he believed what he'd said.

She was insensibly cheered by the statement— insensibly because there was no evidence that he wasn't dead either—but she knew he was a creature of logic and she simply couldn't think straight after everything that had happened.

He shifted around to settle her on the bed. "You should rest. Tomorrow, you will feel more like tackling the problem if you rest now."

She nodded, but she didn't want to be alone—not now.

Truthfully, she had spent so much time alone that it was like a friend to her now and she was usually comfortable with it.

Now—she was afraid of her thoughts and she knew if he left her alone they would crowd close to haunt her. Whatever had happened was not her fault. She knew it wasn't. And yet guilt plagued her.

She had fought and defied him every day of her life and

if he was dead she would never have the chance to say she loved him.

Maybe that didn't matter to him. She'd never believed it did, but it mattered to her.

She needed to say it to him because she hadn't in her memory and she felt like, maybe, that was why he'd never told her that he cared about her. Maybe if she took that first step, she would finally get the love she'd always wanted?

Caleb brought her a glass of water.

Pleased, she sat up and took it and drained the glass. "Thank you! I was so thirsty."

He nodded. "You have lost a lot of fluid weeping so long."

Tabitha bit her lip but couldn't prevent a small chuckle. "Thanks. Was it that bad?"

"Yes. Very bad," he responded seriously. "I am not certain that I will regain full hearing in that ear."

She stared at him a long moment and finally chuckled. "You're teasing."

He looked pleased as he took the glass. "I was. I have not tried that before."

She patted the bed beside her when he looked like he might leave. "Stay with me? At least until I fall asleep? I just … I don't want to be alone."

He looked surprised and confused but happy to oblige. She scooted across the bed and he settled beside her, slipped an arm under her shoulders, and brought her across his chest.

Tabitha was surprised at the move—even though he'd cuddled her already—but she was happy to have even the semblance of tenderness when her emotions were so bruised. She settled her cheek against his shoulder, curled an arm around him, and composed herself for sleep.

After a few moments, Caleb began to stroke a hand down her back, lightly, soothingly.

It did soothe.

But it also made her more aware of the intimacy of their position.

She might be fully clothed.

But Caleb was fully naked—and male and a pleasure model besides.

"May I ask you something?" he asked after a few minutes.

"What?" Tabitha responded cautiously.

He hesitated so long she almost dozed off.

"Why did you never come back to me, baby? I was certain that I had pleased you and that you would come back and ask for me …."

Tabitha abruptly felt like crying all over again.

He could not have a sense of time as she did. Although naturally he had an internal clock, he wasn't mortal and time had little meaning to him beyond the hour of the day—or night—and the tasks assigned to those hours.

How long had he waited? Expecting her to return?

He was a machine. She tried to tell herself that he couldn't have been hurt, but the question itself seemed to belie that belief.

"I couldn't," she said finally, realizing that it wouldn't be a lie to say that she probably would have visited him again. If she'd had the chance, the night he'd given her would have drawn her back to him. "My father was furious when Raathe returned me. He set Raathe to guard me through the night and sent me away the following morning to a …. Well, I always thought of it as a prison. It was a place for wayward teen girls and although we had bedrooms, not cells, we weren't allowed to leave the compound and were rarely even allowed outside of the main building.

"I finished high school there and then I was sent away to college.

"By the time I graduated, I wasn't so focused on

punishing my father as I was in establishing my own life so that I could tell him to go to hell, could be completely independent and free of him."

She shrugged. "And then I came to work in the company he runs. There aren't a lot of jobs to be had so I didn't have much choice, but at least I don't actually work under him—not directly—so I hardly ever see him or have to deal with him anymore."

And she never would—ever again—if he'd been killed.

Caleb distracted her by lifting the hand he'd been caressing her with to her cheek. She glanced at him when he did, just in time to meet the descent of his lips.

His kiss was tender, a supplication rather than conquest as Raathe's kiss had been, but it awakened every nerve and hair follicle.

It reminded her body of his possession before.

How, she wondered dizzily, had she managed to confine this memory to the dark hole in her mind, the place where memories were sent to die?

Or had she simply packed it away with the bittersweet memories that brought as much pain with them as joy when she brought them out?

She thought maybe it was that, because she knew the feel of his lips, his taste, and scent as sharply, as clearly, as if it had only been the day before that she had escaped her father and fled to him to experience 'life'.

And regardless of what her father had said to shame her she had never regretted going to him.

He had been so gentle with her, so careful, that she had experienced nothing but pleasure, unadulterated by more than a hint of pain when he'd pierced her hymen.

She was certain she wouldn't have gotten that otherwise.

Because she hadn't—not since.

Until Raathe ....

She thrust that intrusive thought aside and clutched at Caleb and kissed him back when he seemed on the point of withdrawing.

He hesitated, and then the entire tenor of his kiss, his touch, changed dramatically.

He unleashed his passion upon her. She felt his hunger, his desperation to fill his senses with her in his kiss. His kiss became a powerful mock mating that revved her heart to the point that she was struggling to catch her breath.

And when he broke the kiss at last, it was to strip her clothing off piece by piece, exploring her most tender places as he unveiled them. Within a matter of moments he had set her on fire for him, made her desperate to be claimed.

Fevered, just shy of delirious with the heat he'd generated inside of her, she struggled to give, to fill her hands with the feel of his taut flesh, to caress and stroke him.

That seemed to inspire him.

He massaged her breasts and sucked and pulled at her nipples until she felt like she was going to pass out and began pulling at his hair.

"Caleb!" she said a little desperately when she failed to pry him loose.

His head jerked up. He stared at her for a moment, his eyes glazed, and then abruptly shifted upward to plant his mouth on hers again.

Dismay flickered through her but fortunately she felt his hands skim her hips, pushing at her thighs in a demand that she open them for him.

She did, gladly, desperately and when he rolled into the cradle of her thighs a sense of anticipation swelled inside of her that left her panting and gasping even before he managed to breach the mouth of her sex.

He rose up on his braced arms as he pushed past that boundary and began the journey of claiming. She could feel that he was studying her face. She managed to pry her eyelids up just enough to confirm, but the pressure of his entry was so exquisite she couldn't maintain eye contact. She had to close the world away so that she could fully relish the sense of becoming one with him, treasure the heated abrasion of his flesh as it conquered hers.

She sighed blissfully when she felt the head of his cock come to rest against her womb.

"Baby," Caleb growled, lowering himself until he had pressed his skin against hers from breast to mons and then kissing her in a mock mating of thrusting tongues that nearly brought her off.

He broke off abruptly, lifted his hips so that his cock nearly glided all the way out of her channel and then drove into her again and set a pace that pushed her up the mountain and over the top in a matter of seconds. She sucked in a sharp gasp that bordered a scream as she flew off, wracked by the rapturous convulsions until she was skating the edge of darkness.

He slowed when she came, driving slowly but deeply until the last of the tremors abated and then setting the pace of before.

Doubt flickered through her.

It felt good, but she was more inclined to want to sleep—for a handful of moments. And then the heat caught her up again, lifted her higher. When she reached crisis the second time, it was set off by his climax—the change in rhythm and depth to less than perfect rhythm and deeper thrusts when his body peaked and he was wracked by his own pleasurable convulsions.

She hugged herself tightly to him to ride out the eruption and then drifted lazily toward oblivion in the blissful aftermath.

It occurred to her, though, just before the darkness swallowed her, that he'd climaxed.

Raathe had cum.

And neither of them were real men. Neither were supposed to be capable of what they'd both done with her.

Was it some new programming upgrade to make them more realistic? Or something she should be worried about, she wondered?

Had she finally gone off the deep end as her father had accused her of before? So completely lost touch with reality that she couldn't tell the difference anymore between fantasy and reality?

* * * *

Korbin's dark brows rose. "What has caused you to believe this may be the case?"

Paranoia? Instinct? He had no real idea what had made him decide that he was experiencing death pains, only that he was growing more certain of it and more concerned about Tabitha's welfare if it turned out he was right. "Stabbing pains in my brain. Memories that are not true memories. Dreams of places I have never been and battles I have not fought."

Korbin frowned. "You were not given nanos for such things? I was designed to render aid to injured humans on the battlefield, our handlers—not to make repairs to cyborgs. We are all given the nanos to affect repairs as needed. But, I confess, I am not familiar with the CHS series at all."

"In the beginning—no. I was told that that was one of the upgrades that was done the first time my master sent me back to the company. But my dealings with Mr. Langston have led me to expect treachery. He appears to feel no loyalty to anyone—even Tabitha. I would not put it past him to have had a self-destruct embedded."

"I see nothing in the scan beyond a bit of scar tissue that I would not have expected. What would trigger the self-destruct if you are correct?"

Raathe sat up. "I have no idea."

"When did this first start?"

Raathe thought about it. He had been inclined to associate the pain with the awakening, but he realized as he probed old memories that that was not the case. "It was not long after I was assigned as Mr. Langston's Cybernetic Home Security," he said slowly, struggling to summon the memory. "Tabby was a small child then. She had disappeared and I was given the task of finding her."

"And you had not experienced this before that time? What about afterward? How long afterward before you had another ... episode?"

Raathe considered for a far longer time and finally reached a conclusion that was less than satisfactory. "They were more frequent when Tabby was in trouble," he said a little hesitantly. "It is almost as if that triggered the attacks."

Korbin thought that over. "That is ... very illogical. We have only just awakened and before the awakening we were unable to process like humans, unable to experience emotions. I cannot believe that you awakened so long before everyone else."

Raathe stared at him. "I did not. It was not long ago at all. I am as certain as I can be that it coincided with everyone else's awakening."

"Well, that makes less sense," Korbin said irritably. "The symptoms you describe fit a human reaction to stress—excessive, but, as described, it still fits. You should not have had any reaction at all, though, before the awakening. So this does not make sense. And yet, neither can I dismiss it. Not altogether, at any rate." He frowned. "Mayhap it was a simulated effect that triggered an actual one? Some sort of defect. You are the first of your kind, yes? The 300s were the original model. There may have been bugs that were worked out with later models and perhaps that is also why your master sent you for upgrades? But then it was not entirely successful?"

Raathe gave him a look. "So ... you are saying you cannot tell me with any certainty whether this is terminal or not or pin down what might be causing it?"

Korbin considered the question long and hard. "Yes. That is what I am saying."

"That is so fucking helpful," Raathe growled, climbing off of the examination table and stalking from the room. He hesitated once outside, but the truth was that he was bone weary.

He had never experienced that particular feeling before the awakening.

He had felt drained of energy when he had not been able to renew his source at the proper times, but it had been a different sort of weakening than what he felt now.

He did not recall feeling that he must rest. He had done so to conserve energy in the past, but that was a logical balance of resources. He consumed x amount for x amount of output and he conserved that energy when he did not need to expend it by going into sleep mode.

He was changed—without his desire or seeking it—he had been changed radically and permanently.

It remained to be seen if it was something he would grow accustomed to, let alone take any pleasure in ….

But that thought brought him to what had transpired between him and Tabby in the shower.

That had pleasured him almost to the point that he thought he might expire in that moment.

He did not even know why he had done it.

It had simply been an uncontrollable urge.

Not that he regretted it.

What he regretted, deeply, was that he might have given her a disgust of him and that she would never allow him to touch her that way again.

He suspected she had turned from him and taken Caleb as her lover, but he did not think it would be safe to investigate that and possibly discover that he was right at this point.

He did not trust himself to deal with it with any semblance of reason.

It would be best to rest now, he thought. Then, perhaps, he would be able to see things more clearly so he could decide what would be best for Tabitha in the event that he terminated and could not continue to take care of her.

And he thought that he must rest to have a clear head if they were facing a fight.

And he was fairly certain they were.

That depended, of course, on whether he had managed to convince the authorities that they had left the area by sending the drones out to destroy evidence of their passing as appeared to be the case. He had no real fear that they would be able to get past the security Langston had installed, but they could not stay below ground in the shelter forever. They would have to come up and there was no telling what they might have to face when they did.

That being the case, his preference would be to leave as soon as possible, to make every effort to keep from exposing Tabitha to possible harm.

The question was, where might be a safe place in a universe controlled by big business? When they were, to all intents and purposes, only one giant corporation.

* * * *

As was so often the case, when the music died, common sense resurrected its untimely head.

Uneasiness began to creep into Tabitha's subconscious long before she reached the upper levels of awareness, she supposed due to the furnace she was sleeping beside that was … snoring—not deafeningly—but still ….

That discovery threw her into a state of panic that precluded logical brain function for a time. All she could do was race around in circles trying to catch an elusive memory that ran faster than she could.

Eventually, the events of the day before and more specifically the night before finally emerged from the depths to horrify her.

Her father was lost—maybe dead—and she had spent

the night with the pleasure droid—who had fucked her brains out and then fallen asleep beside her just like a real man generally did. Or at least the real men that she'd had close contact with.

Both of them.

But this wasn't a real man. It was Caleb—her first—the pleasure droid she had gone to to dispose of her virginity because some girl at school had said that her mother had said that that was way better than throwing it away on a human male—especially a very young one who would only be interested in his own pleasure.

Of course, poor Caleb had been second choice.

Not that she could see that he had any reason to be upset about that even if he *could* be upset about it.

Which he couldn't.

It was really strange, though, that Raathe and Caleb in particular seemed to be behaving as if they *were* able to feel a very great deal on the subject.

Was there any possibility, she wondered, that they had received the new programming patch?

But if that was the case why would they then have been put down in the pens to be put down?

And what in the world could they have been thinking to add a programming patch that made the cyborgs *that* realistic?

It didn't make sense. Really, it didn't. So what was she to think?

Chapter Eight

Raathe hesitated outside the bedroom where Tabitha had slept the night before, wrestling with his temper.

He had searched every bedroom, though, and Caleb was not to be found and he could not tell that he had slept in any of the bedrooms.

Actually, Korbin had also not slept in one of the bedrooms and it flickered through his mind to wonder if he was the only one who had *not* fucked Tabitha the night before.

Deciding to at least attempt the behavior of a sane person, he turned away from the door and headed downstairs. There he found Korbin staring bleary eyed at the security monitors.

Relieved of his dark suspicions regarding Korbin, at least, he paused to study the monitors himself. "I will take watch so that you can rest."

Korbin glanced at him, lifted one dark eyebrow at the clothing he had appropriated from his master's closet, and nodded. "I believe I will look for food first," he said, pushing himself to his feet and then stretching.

Raathe's stomach complained. "That is what I am missing," he murmured in agreement. "But I am looking for that asshole, Caleb."

Korbin refrained from flicking a glance in the direction of Tabitha's bedroom with an effort. "I have not seen him since last eve."

Raathe studied him with suspicion but finally simply nodded and began a systematic search of the lower level of the bunker/mansion. Korbin followed him rather than heading to bed or the kitchen, but Raathe ignored him.

It occurred to him once he'd searched the entire residence, that he had not checked the hanger and with uneasiness riding him, he strode quickly to the hanger.

Thankfully, Langston's private cruiser was still in the

hanger, but the ramp was extended and the main cabin door standing open.

Frowning, he flicked a questioning glance at Korbin and then crossed the hanger and jogged up the ramp.

The ship was empty of habitation, but there was clear evidence that it had been prepped for a lengthy voyage—or at least someone had been in the process of doing so.

"Her father was leaving," Korbin stated the obvious.

"It seems so," Raathe responded thoughtfully.

"The ship's log reports preparations for two—one male and one female."

"Yes," Raathe responded. "The question is—were the preparations for Tabitha? Or his girlfriend?"

They headed back to the residence after they discovered what they could and found Tabitha in the kitchen preparing food.

Caleb, also dapper in a suit that was Langston's property if not his personal attire, had his ass parked in *his* chair, Raathe decided, since it was adjacent to Tabitha's.

He strode across the room and snatched the chair out from under him.

Naturally enough, Caleb hit the floor.

"Cut it out!" Tabitha snapped. "I haven't even had my damned coffee yet! I can't handle the roughhousing right now!"

Raathe narrowed his eyes at Caleb and sat in the chair he'd emptied.

Tabitha hesitated and then set the plate she'd brought for Caleb down in front of Raathe and returned to the food processor to key in an order for two more breakfast plates.

"You are only eating toast?" Raathe demanded disapprovingly. "It is no wonder that you are mostly bones."

Caleb punched his shoulder when he saw Tabitha's hurt, angry expression. "She is beautiful."

Raathe clocked Caleb on the jaw, knocking him out of

the chair he'd just seated himself in. "Of course she is beautiful," he growled. "But she is too thin."

The comment dried up the tears that had stung her eyes, but she was skeptical now that Raathe believed that after the other comment.

Then she took herself to task for reacting to the insult or the compliment. They were making observations—both of them.

Sure the truth hurt sometimes, but she should be mostly immune to such things considering her upbringing.

They were behaving like … juveniles, she decided. Completely mature adults one moment and squabbling like children the next.

She considered that thoughtfully as she settled to drink her coffee and nibble the cold toast and realized that that assessment was actually a pretty close assessment of what she'd observed.

What, she wondered, would cause that sort of behavioral issues? Some sort of corruption of the logic circuits?

She supposed she really ought to take them down to the med center and do a thorough scan on all three of them, but it was just going to have to wait until she discovered what she could about her father.

Leaving the three guys wolfing down the huge breakfasts she'd ordered for them, she headed into her father's office and sat down at his desk.

Not surprised in the least when she discovered she was locked out of the system, she began a search of the office for the codes she knew her father would have hidden. She was bent over, struggling to see the bottom of the desk when someone grasped her hips in two huge hands and nearly shoved her under the desk when he began pounding his pelvis against her ass.

Fighting her way free, she whirled on the cyborg behind her and punched him on one shoulder, careful not to hit him hard enough to hurt her hand. "Damn it, Korbin! What the hell was that? And don't tell me you were examining me for injury, damn it! I didn't believe it last time and I damned sure don't believe *that* was what that was!"

He stared at her with an expression she found difficult to interpret—anger certainly, guilt, embarrassment, disappointment and maybe a smidgeon of confusion as to why he had decided he wanted to become a pleasure droid. Or maybe the confusion was that he hadn't gotten any part of the action?

"I want to fuck."

Tabitha gaped at him, blinking as she tried to absorb and interpret what he'd said.

But there was no interpretation needed. It was damned straightforward. "You want to fuck?"

"Yes."

Raathe grabbed him by the hair and dragged him out of the office before she could think of a suitable reply.

"You stupid fuck!" Caleb growled. "You do not ask a lady to fuck!"

Someone punched him in the mouth and he staggered backwards past the office door.

"OK, damn it! You're going to have to fix whatever you break! And clean up the mess because I'm damned sure not cleaning it up!" she yelled after them.

She settled in the desk chair again as the battle moved down the hallway and tried the code she'd found just before Korbin tried to hide his salami in her heavenly gate.

She couldn't decide whether he thought he was supposed to pleasure her because Raathe and Caleb had or he was just trying to make himself useful.

Shaking off her lingering doubts when the code unlocked the system, she pulled up the security footage of the shelter.

What she discovered was far more disturbing than she'd expected.

Korbin had accessed the security system and watched

her and Caleb together—which explained, she supposed, his sudden interest in fucking.

But as disturbing as that was, it paled beside the discovery of what had taken place in the med center while she was fucking Caleb.

Raathe thought he might be dying?

He couldn't be dying.

She felt a knot the size of her fist gather in her throat until she could barely swallow and her chest tightened until every breath was painful.

Why hadn't he come to her with his suspicions?

She could have taken him in to have him examined for problems!

Now they were cut off from the factory and she wouldn't have any way to fix a problem even if she could find whatever it was!

She was so focused on her thoughts she didn't even know when the sounds of battle finally petered out.

She didn't know how long Raathe had been standing in the doorway when she finally became aware of his presence.

Blinking away the tears that had filled her eyes, she quickly changed the date on the videos to the day before they'd arrived. And when Raathe rounded the desk and glanced at the screen, he saw her father moving around the residence.

He crouched beside her and studied her face earnestly. "Do not despair, Tabby. I will find him for you."

Tabitha sniffed, struggling with the effort to dismiss her urge to cry.

It would … unsettle him and confuse him. He wasn't programmed to deal with that sort of thing.

Still, she couldn't resist lifting a hand to stroke his hard cheek. "You know that you're more …." She stopped abruptly, realizing what she'd almost said.

Horrified, she allowed her hand to fall away, swallowed

against the knot of sorrow in her throat and looked away. "Yes. I know that if it's possible, you will."

She wouldn't meet his gaze even when he captured her face and forced her to look toward him. "Tell me, Tabby. What is it? Whatever I can do to fix it, I will."

In the end, she discovered she just couldn't contain her grief completely. She put her arms around his shoulders and burrowed her face against his throat. "Don't leave me, Raathe—ever. Promise?"

He held her a moment and then gently pulled her arms away. "You saw the vid," he said flatly.

She bit her lip, but she neither confirmed nor denied.

She saw she didn't need to.

He shook his head at her. "I will always do my utmost not to fail you. I will give you that promise."

That wasn't good enough, damn it! But she realized that even he couldn't promise more than that.

"Now … let me see what you have discovered."

Tabitha flicked a glance toward the doorway and saw that Caleb and Korbin had joined them. She met Caleb's gaze for a long moment as she brought up the video beginning prior to their arrival in the shelter—wished that she'd had the time and presence of mind to delete it—better suspicions about *why* it had been deleted than for him to actually see why she had.

Raathe and Korbin had already fought. She saw no sense in risking another incident by allowing Raathe to see the video of her and Caleb together … or the one where Korbin watched them.

They would spend the remainder of the day arguing and brawling about it if they ran true to form.

Well, recent behavior.

Raathe hadn't been prone to that before—although he had certainly disposed of her high school crush and Caleb without regard to damaging them.

Because there were no other cyborgs around, she

supposed, for him to take exception to—so no opportunity for him to display the aggressive behavior.

Or maybe no reason to develop it until he'd been penned up with them for days?

Raathe shifted closer. "This is the night before Mr. Langston went missing?"

"Yes."

Raathe hesitated, watching Langston's movements in the office and around the residence before he spoke. "He did not come to the shelter to prepare for a trip to the main office. In fact, I am not convinced that he intended to go there any of the time. He has prepped his private cruiser for a very long voyage."

Tabitha whipped a shocked, hopeful glance at him. "You think he might have … faked his death?"

Surprise flickered in his eyes, but Raathe shook his head. "I could not presume that to be the case. But he was aware that there was trouble, I believe, and that he might need to flee. He removed his tracker and I would think that is not only a powerful indication that he meant to disappear but also of the level of danger he felt. And since that was clearly his intention all along, then we cannot say that the police are correct and something has happened to him. It is just as possible that that was part of the plan all along—that he staged a very public kidnapping to convince everyone that he was dead when he disappeared."

"Do you think that you could get into the computer at the police station and see what they have?"

Raathe nodded. "I can try to bypass their security."

"I will see if I can hack into the military satellite system," Korbin offered, pushing away from the doorframe. "There could be something that they picked up."

Raathe did, in fact, manage to pull up the files the cops had compiled on the case and they were able to read the report and see the crime scene pictures.

They were gory. Tabitha had a hard time believing they were staged—any part of it—because his body guards had been killed and both of them were human.

Surely her father wouldn't have set them up to die?

"Maybe this was merely a diversion and it went wrong?" Raathe offered after a few moments.

That meant it had occurred to him that her father might have sacrificed the guards for his greater good.

And, if she was honest, she knew he was capable of it. Or at least believed he could be.

Korbin summoned them after a little bit to see the images he had managed to capture from the satellite and they were able to see fairly clearly that her father had left the vehicle on his own two feet after the attack—alone, not as a captive.

As much as Tabitha hated to admit it, even to herself, that certainly seemed to point to the set-up theory.

They couldn't see what was happening inside the vehicle, but they also couldn't see any attackers from outside.

"It might have been long range snipers—or drone mounted snipers—that took out the guards," Korbin offered.

Tabitha studied his expression for several moments and finally nodded.

He didn't believe that and she didn't.

She also couldn't convince herself that her father had reacted to an attack inside the vehicle by men who'd turned on him, but there was at least a possibility that that was the case. She owed it to her father to at least give him the benefit of a doubt.

* * * *

Tabitha spent most of the day wrestling with the facts that she had and trying to put them together and into perspective. By that evening she realized that she just didn't know her father well enough to feel confident she knew what he would do—and wouldn't. And that made it impossible to guess what he would do now.

Heading into the kitchen, she studied the possibilities and put together a meal.

While she waited for the food processor to do its thing, she leaned against the counter, thinking.

One by one the guys arrived, drawn by the smells emanating from the machine as it cooked the dishes she'd programmed into it.

Raathe was last.

He gave poor Caleb a dark look. Caleb, without acknowledging in any way that he noticed, got up and moved to another place.

Tabitha was tempted to move her place setting to the seat beside Caleb, but decided against stirring up trouble.

It seemed very likely it would.

In any case, she supposed they were like people in that sense—they established a pecking order and expected it to be followed.

Maybe she just hadn't observed the cyborgs interacting enough to know what to expect, she thought abruptly? That would certainly explain the 'strange' behavior she thought she was seeing.

"We have finished prepping your father's cruiser for two extra passengers," Raathe announced once Tabitha had taken the dishes out and set them on the table so that everyone could help themselves.

Tabitha sat, frowning as she did a quick calculation. "It was prepped for two?"

Raathe sent Korbin a speaking look. "Yes. We supposed for you and your father."

Tabitha stared at him. "You think Father meant to take me with him?" she asked, not even attempting to hide her dismay.

The three males exchanged confused looks. "Yes?" Raathe replied finally, a questioning lilt of uncertainty belying his assertion.

Tabitha considered it. "Seems more likely that he would have prepared for his girlfriend," she responded, helping herself to the cauliflower dish she'd prepared and then pushing the bowl toward Raathe and slicing the beef roast. "I don't see him thinking I'd go willingly—maybe if he had me bound and gagged. I don't think I've actually spoken to him—except as my boss—in a year. I mean had an actual conversation."

She thought about that a few moments while they passed the dishes around and served themselves and was abruptly excited at the possibility of a breakthrough. "I'll *bet* that was why he was out there!"

She glanced around at the men. "That explains why he didn't just leave! He went to get Carol!"

Raathe frowned thoughtfully. "Why would he not simply tell her to come here?"

"Hmmm. You're right. That sounds much more like that inconsiderate bastard." She thought it over. "Maybe he couldn't convince her to come? She was-is—pretty timid—very submissive. I'm sure that's what he liked about her, but even so, she could have balked at following orders that had the potential for putting her in harm's way.

"But maybe the faked death was part of that? Maybe he had already figured it wasn't going to do the trick to just run? He had to convince everyone he was dead. So he arranged to pick her up somewhere—or dragged her into it by telling her she had to pick him up after he'd set up the kidnap?

"I bet that was it! I bet that was exactly it!"

"So ... we are waiting for your father to arrive?" Caleb asked hesitantly.

"Oh! He would be soooo pissed off if we took off with his ship!" Tabitha said, struggling with her delight at the fantasy of his expression if he discovered she'd done such a thing. "I'd be tempted to take off without him, too, but he must be in to something pretty bad to hatch this kind of crazy plot."

"What do you think that he is in to?" Korbin asked curiously.

Tabitha shook her head. "No clue, honestly, but bad. Must have to do with dirty dealings with the government, though."

"Why do you say that?"

Tabitha abruptly remembered that Korbin was a CO. She didn't know how that little factoid could have slipped her mind. "Well, they did a massive recall on the COs they'd sold to the government for their pet war. Not saying *you* have a problem," she added quickly, "but something is up with that. I couldn't find out what. That's what I was doing at the factory when ... well, when I let you guys go. I was trying to track down something specific to explain why they'd done that and why they'd lied about the recall being just something about a programming glitch.

"Of course I don't know positively that that's what this was about. There might not have been any connection at all. It might also have had to do with the step-up in production of factory borgs that has everybody so stirred up.

"I checked everything I got the chance to look at while I was there, but ... nothing really jumped out at me so I'm still in the dark about the 'why'."

"But I do think we need to assume that he'll be coming back to collect the ship since he prepped it and we need to go ahead and make sure there are enough supplies for six."

"We are leaving?" Caleb asked, clearly happy at the thought.

Raathe glared at him. "Your father will not accept those two," he said flatly. "And certainly not me."

Tabitha gaped at him. "What do you mean 'certainly not you'?"

He studied her for a long moment. "How do you think

that I got into the pens?"

Tabitha felt the blood leave her face. "You're saying …? Father knew?"

His lips tightened. "Your father signed the order."

Tabitha simply couldn't take that in and process it. It wasn't as if it hadn't crossed her mind, but she didn't want to believe her father was that cold blooded. Of course, they'd never seen eye to eye on the cyborgs. Technically, they weren't human even though the biological material used to construct them, or most of it, *was* human. They were hybrids. Even the biological materials used to build them were grown in the lab, and they were less that 50% biological entity, by law.

But Tabitha had never been able to simply dismiss them as machines and that was the only way her father saw them.

It still didn't make sense to her, but she knew Raathe was incapable of lying.

"That bastard! Well, we damned sure aren't leaving anybody behind! The cops are just waiting to get in here. And I'm not going to jail for releasing you guys when you shouldn't have been in the pens to start with! And I'm damned sure not letting them take you off and destroy you!"

Chapter Nine

Not that they could tell from the bunker since there were no windows, but it was barely dawn when Korbin summoned them downstairs to where he had stationed himself at the monitor wall to track threats from outside. Her internal clock was still set to the natural rhythm, however, and it was all she could do to lever herself out of her bed, let alone think.

Korbin had said it was critical, however, and she stumbled from her bed and made a stab at wakeup grooming and then dragged a robe around her shoulders and wove a drunken path downstairs.

By the time she got there all three of the guys were hovering by the monitors, completely focused on what appeared to be rolling fog or maybe a dust cloud in the distance.

Her eyes still burning from being awakened so abruptly, she blinked over and over trying to clear her vision and peered hard at first one screen and then another.

"What is it?" she asked finally.

"Protestors from the city," Raathe said grimly.

Tabitha's eyes widened and her heart rate shot up a couple of notches, bringing her closer to complete consciousness. "Headed this way?" she asked blankly. "Why in the world would they be out here? This far from town?"

Raathe and Korbin exchanged a long look.

"To be more precise," Korbin corrected himself, "these are people who *were* protesting. I do not think they are headed to your father's compound to protest. I believe they have moved past the protesting and past the riots to full-fledged revolt. They are armed."

Tabitha digested that with an effort. "So ... you're saying this is a ... revolt?"

"I believe so," Raathe answered that time. "The cops

are pulling out."

That jolted Tabitha. "Those *bastards*! Now that they're needed to guard the place, they tuck tail and run?"

"To be completely fair," Caleb said placatingly, "they *are* outnumbered."

"Yeah, but damn it we're a lot more outnumbered than they are!"

"We are in the bunker. We are protected," Korbin said.

"Yes, but for how long? If they're armed …. And we don't know what all they might have to throw at us. They could've gotten military weapons, grenades, bombs—no telling what. You think they'd believe us if we told them my father isn't here?"

Korbin studied her for a long moment.

"I don't think so either. Well, I need coffee," she said, turning away and heading toward the kitchen. She'd barely gotten a cup made when the guys trooped in and sat down at the table. She frowned at them, but instead of telling them to use the food processor to make their own damned breakfast, she shrugged inwardly and moved to the machine to select an assortment of breakfast items and programmed it to cook.

She considered the situation while she waited, sipping her coffee. About the time the chime sounded, alerting her to the fact that the meal was cooked, the caffeine in her coffee kicked in and she arrived at the only decision she could have made.

"I think we should just go," Tabitha announced as she settled at the table.

The guys all seemed to relax instantly—just an impression, but she thought they did.

Odd that she hadn't actually noticed that they were tense before.

"The cruiser is fully prepped," Raathe said.

"More than ready since your father and his girlfriend will not be coming," Caleb pointed out cheerfully.

Raathe punched him in the ribs, driving the air from his lungs and the bite of food he'd just taken out of his mouth with enough force it arched in the air and landed in the center of the table, barely missing the plate of eggs.

"Eew!" Tabitha said disapprovingly. "It's very bad manners to spit on the table and I feel queasy enough first thing in the morning without seeing that."

She was sorry she'd said anything when she saw how red Caleb turned with discomfort, but really! Nasty!

He begged pardon through gritted teeth and wiped the offense from the table with his napkin.

"Anyway, where was I? Oh! Well, I've thought about it and I think father would have beaten us here if he hadn't had to change plans. I'm convinced he went to plan B and we needn't worry about him."

Actually, Tabitha wasn't convinced—not nearly as certain as she would have liked to be. But she didn't see that endangering themselves was going to help her father and she knew him well enough to know that he always did have backup plans in case anything went wrong. He *expected* problems to come up, plans to go awry. That much was true and it was the main reason she was almost a hundred percent certain that they would be risking everything when he would most likely be fine without their help—wouldn't have counted on it at all.

He was a grown man and had been taking care of himself for a very long time.

She was the one that was woefully inexperienced.

Her father had suffocated her her entire life—had her under guard or virtually imprisoned until she'd had very little chance to gain life experience.

And, of course, none at all in this type of situation!

And she *had* questioned whether she was just jumping at the chance to escape a situation she knew she wasn't competent to handle or if she believed, deep in her heart of hearts, that she was doing the only thing she could.

She felt guilty about leaving, but she thought she would have even if there was no room for doubt about her father's situation. She didn't think it was actually a reaction to knowingly acting in the wrong.

And, truthfully, the decision was almost entirely because of the guys.

She was pretty sure she would be ok.

She was as certain as she needed to be that they wouldn't be ok and that was the real kicker.

She knew she couldn't live with herself if she was determined to stay and everything went very wrong and the guys paid for it.

She couldn't even bear thinking about it.

Korbin was relieved on all counts.

He had pledged his life to Tabitha and he did not mind giving it up if it was to further his vow to her, but he did not see that there was anything that he could do to protect Tabitha from the mob outside. It was far too reminiscent of the disaster on Xeno-12 where they had been overrun by the enemy. There were far too many of them for anything short of an equal, opposing force to contend with, with any possibility of success.

Even with Raathe and Caleb both fighting beside him, that only meant the three of them were facing termination—not an increase in the odds of winning. And he knew they would. They were as devoted to protecting Tabitha as he was.

And failure could mean Tabitha would lose her life.

He did not believe that she was their target, but he also did not believe that that would make any difference to a mob like the one approaching. They had left reason behind.

The arrival of her father would have complicated an already difficult situation. He was certain that Raathe knew the man well enough to make a judgment and if he thought the father would demand they stay behind that was probably the way it would go down.

And then he would have to prevent Tabitha from going—putting her in more danger—or he would have to force his way onto the ship—and she would probably not be happy if he terminated her father for getting in his way.

No, leaving now was the best case scenario—if they could manage it before Tabitha had time to think more and perhaps change her mind.

* * * *

Tabitha had cleaned up the kitchen and the eating area before it occurred to her that not only was it probably pointless when they were leaving anyway, but she had cleaned up after them when they were perfectly capable of doing it themselves.

And they had merely stood and watched as if … maybe too stunned to move if they'd been human?

Putting it down to distraction and shaking it, she headed out of the area to check the monitors again.

The crowd was much closer now. Close enough that she could make out individuals in the seething mass, see that they were indeed carrying weapons of all kinds.

One even had a bazooka—not good. The front gates were designed to take a direct hit from something that powerful, but they would not hold up to a repeated, determined assault.

Leaving the monitors, she headed down the hallway that led to the hanger and climbed the gangplank.

The guys, she saw, were already inside checking the stock.

The cruiser was a luxury model. It had a very large master cabin and two smaller cabins for guests.

They would have to rotate sleeping arrangements, but she saw no reason why she shouldn't move her personal belongings into the master cabin.

Not that she had a great deal since she'd had to evacuate her apartment in just the clothes on her back, but there were personal things in the mansion from the time before she'd moved out.

She discovered Raathe's uniforms were in the clothing locker when she opened it—and the suit he'd discarded from earlier. Her heart did a little tap dance at that discovery, but she shrugged it off. She'd already realized they would have to rotate sleeping times.

If it came to that, she didn't suppose there was any reason why she couldn't sleep in the same bed with Raathe.

He was completely familiar to her. It might feel a little strange since she was accustomed to sleeping alone, but she thought she could adjust to it if it transpired that was necessary.

Dismissing that for the moment, she headed out of the ship again and returned to the main residence and then took the elevator up to the mansion.

As soon as the doors opened at the top she could hear the noise of the mob.

Goose bumps erupted all over her arms and climbed her neck.

Trying to shake the fear that had suddenly gripped her, she moved to a window overlooking the front gate and peered out.

That was when she discovered that the crowd was a *lot* closer than she'd thought they would be. Spurred by that discovery, she whirled away from the window and raced to the room that she still considered hers even though she hadn't even paid lip service to living with her father in years. When she reached the room, she headed straight to the closet and snatched a travel bag from it and then began to grab things at random and shove them in.

She was loading a second bag when all three of the guys arrived, sounding like a herd of buffalos as they jogged down the hall and into her room.

"Oh my god!" Tabitha gasped. "I thought the mob had breached the wall and were coming for me."

Raathe's lips tightened. "And this is why you continue to pack?"

She looked down at the high heel shoes in her hand. "I packed faster," she said meekly.

Shaking his head, Raathe snatched her up and jogged from the room.

"My stuff! Damn it Raathe!"

"We have it!" Korbin offered, racing behind them with one of the bags.

Caleb grinned at her and showed her he'd grabbed the other.

He hadn't zipped it, though, and he was leaving a trail of her belongings behind him.

Damn it!

Tabitha dismissed her annoyance abruptly when she heard the sound of breaking glass. Almost instantly, noxious smoke began to fill the hallway.

"Teargas," Korbin said succinctly.

They ran the last few yards to the elevator and dove into the cubicle. Raathe punched the buttons and the doors closed and the cubicle began a swift descent.

"You can put me down now," Tabitha said with a sigh of relief.

Raathe met her gaze, struggled to think of something to say that would not offend, and finally gave up. "You are too slow and I cannot risk that you will be diverted to search for other useless things. The ship is fully prepped and ready for launch."

Tabitha gaped at him. "I know you did not just insult me!" she managed to gasp after a moment.

"Good," Raathe responded. "I thought you might take exception, but I could not think how I might sugar coat the truth to make it more palatable. I was not given social protocol programming."

That left Tabitha at a complete loss for words. They were halfway down the corridor that led to the hanger before she recovered sufficiently to object, but when she realized they had nearly reached their objective she dismissed it. She satisfied her sense of misuse by giving him the cold shoulder once he had set her on her feet and stalking off to the master cabin.

It was a shame, she thought, that she couldn't slam the damn door! The automatic sliding doors eliminated any possibility of satisfaction in that direction.

She had plopped down on the bed to sulk when Raathe returned, entering the room without a by-your-leave!

His expression was grim. "We have a problem."

Tabitha lifted her brows questioningly.

"Two actually."

"Ok."

"The mob has breached the security wall."

"Oh," Tabitha gasped, coming to her feet. "Oh my god!"

"And we cannot get the ship's onboard computer to turn over control of the ship."

Tabitha gaped at him in disbelief. "But ... how did you get on board and into the system to check the launch status?"

"I used the tracker your father left. It identified itself as him. However, security protocol for the ship launch requires a secondary ...."

Tabitha strode past him and down the corridor to the ship's cockpit. When she reached it, she saw that Caleb and Korbin were strapped into two of the four passenger seats. "Get into the launch harness," she told Raathe without turning and then plopped into the pilot's seat and grappled with her own harness.

Raathe ignored her and dropped into the seat beside her.

Irritation flickered inside of her and she realized this was something he seemed in the habit of doing—ignoring direct orders from her that he could hardly fail to notice *were* orders.

Of course, he hadn't really been programmed to follow *her* orders.

Dismissing that for the moment, she pulled up the ID screen and allowed the computer to scan her eye.

"Welcome, Mistress Tabitha Langston."

"Hello Lisa. Please check all systems for takeoff."

"Checking."

The computer verbally listed all systems and checked them off one by one.

"We are at peak capacity. Cargo exceeds maximum acceptable weight."

Dismay flickered through Tabitha, but before she could think of what to do, Korbin threw his straps off, picked up the first bag she'd packed, and strode down the corridor.

Tabitha was still trying to figure out what his intention was when he opened the hatch, pitched the bag out, and then closed it and headed back.

"Weight within acceptable limits," the computer announced.

Indignation flooded Tabitha. "You threw out my bag!" she said accusingly when Korbin returned and settled again.

"I did not think it would be logical to throw out a weight equivalent of food. We had calculated that very carefully."

It was hard to argue with that kind of logic. She wanted to, but the problem with that was that she had no idea how much food they would need for the trip and they couldn't eat what she'd packed in her bag.

With an effort, she focused on the launch.

Thankfully, there was no problem opening the bay door.

Unfortunately, it appeared that a handful of the rioters had discovered it.

Unfortunately for them.

Cringing, Tabitha started the engines and when she saw they had a bazooka they were trying to line up to fire, she dismissed her qualms and launched, scorching a trail up the chute to the bay doors. She thought the rioters dove out of the way, but it was not something she wanted to dwell on. If they hadn't managed to escape—well, she hadn't put them in harm's way and she damned well had no intention of letting them shoot the ship to protect those bastards.

She more than half expected the men to fire upon them and blast them to smithereens as they emerged, before they had time to gain altitude, but, thankfully, they didn't manage to collect themselves in time to do any damage.

Loaded to capacity or not, the cruiser was fast and it shot through the atmosphere and into space in a matter of minutes. There were several explosions close enough behind them for the concussion to make the ship shimmy, but not close enough to damage anything.

The artificial gravity engaged automatically—one of the luxury options—increasing as Earth's gravity decreased so that there was virtually no noticeable transition from true gravity to artificial.

Tabitha preferred it that way. Weightlessness held no thrill for her.

Not that she had traveled in space a very great deal beyond the short excursions necessary for her pilot training, but her father had insisted upon introducing her to weightlessness on her first trip out and she'd puked her guts out and she'd had no interest in repeating the experience.

"I did not know that you were trained to pilot the ship," Raathe commented.

Tabitha sent him a quick look and then set the autopilot. "Father liked to have backup plans. He liked backups for his backups," she said with a faint chuckle and then shrugged. "Maybe he was hoping I'd take the ship the next time I decided to run away so he could wash his hands of me for good."

Raathe frowned, realizing that he should say something but with no idea what would be appropriate, truthful, and still be helpful rather than hurtful. "I believe he cared for you as much as he was capable of," he said finally.

Tabitha studied his face, feeling her belly tighten in that odd way it did whenever she allowed herself to look deeply into his eyes. "Maybe," she conceded, "but he didn't have much capacity for it. You always seemed … warmer and that's just sad."

Chapter Ten

Raathe frowned, wondering what she meant by that statement. He was tempted to ask, but he did not like that Caleb and Korbin were listening so he dismissed it—for the time being anyway. "You should train me to pilot the ship."

Tabitha's brows lifted, but it didn't take a lot of extrapolation to realize that he was right. "They should learn, too," she agreed, nodding her head toward Caleb and Korbin. "Better all the way around. And I can program Lisa to accept any of us as pilot if we run into any kind of trouble."

Unfastening her safety harness, she got up and moved to the console beside Korbin. Settling in the seat, she pulled up the pilot's manual. "Y'all can start here. This is how I learned and then, once you have all this in memory, you only need a little practice. The ship mostly flies itself. Father always preferred to handle the landing manually since that's the most dangerous time … well, and take off."

She got up once she'd pulled the manual up. "Was there any of my stuff that wasn't pitched off the ship?"

Korbin ignored the question and wrestled Raathe for the seat she'd vacated.

Caleb smiled at her. "I have the bag that I carried!"

Surprise and happiness washed through Tabitha. "You brought it?"

It wasn't until he led her down the central corridor and took the bag from a locker that she remembered that it hadn't been closed and stuff was spilling out as he ran. She remembered it then because the bag was half empty.

Thanking him, she went into the master cabin, poured the contents out on the bed, and struggled not to cry. There was one and half pairs of high heels in the bag and a wad of stockings, a bra, no panties, and a couple of bottles of hair product.

She had always tried very hard not to focus on the material things—mostly because her father was obsessive about accumulating money and things and she didn't want to be anything like him.

But it was hard to simply dismiss the fact that she'd lost every personal thing she'd owned and wasn't likely to ever see them again.

She was sure she could avoid prosecution if she went to her father's retreat—the destination that had been programmed into the ship's computer. There was no extradition treaty between Destiny and Earth—which was why her father had chosen it for his retreat—and besides that it was on the very outer rim of settled worlds—too far for the authorities to care to follow, she was fairly convinced.

But the very fact that it was so far out meant that it was

really primitive and the living conditions were marginal.

Of course, she was sure she could count on the fact that her father had had it lavishly appointed because he loved luxury, but everything would have been for his benefit, geared towards his needs and desires. It seemed very unlikely he would have stocked the place with things she would need.

Maybe for the girlfriend since it seemed obvious he'd planned to take her?

She might have to wrestle for whatever was there, but it did give her a glimmer of hope.

Thinking about the girlfriend brought to mind that Raathe had said the ship was stocked with things for a woman, but she'd searched the cabin thoroughly when she'd first boarded and she didn't recall seeing a thing—not even toiletries.

Scooping the stuff back into the bag, she set it in the bottom of the clothing locker and went out to ask Raathe what had been done with the things.

* * * *

While Raathe was scanning and storing the information Tabitha had produced, he was listening to the onboard computer, Lisa, communicating with ground computers.

Apparently, Langston had decided to pay a fine for not registering flight plans because that was what ground control was screaming—that he had not filed flight plans and was not authorized to fly and would be fined and possibly jailed if he did not return to port immediately.

And yet there were definitely flight plans.

Lisa had been instructed to fly a brief diversionary path, to make certain no one was following, and then head to Destiny.

"Where is this Destiny?" Korbin asked.

"It is a border world as I understand it," Raathe responded. "I have not been there but Langston was never concerned about discussing anything in front of me and I have heard much about it. He built a shelter there much like the one we just left. It is surrounded by a twenty foot security wall, however, because this place is an ungovernable land, wild and dangerous because it gathers the lawless from all parts of the colonized universe.

"I am thinking this is not a place that we want to take Tabitha. It might be no better than the situation we just escaped—very likely worse."

Korbin frowned. "It is likely to be a place where we could meet with agents from the cyborg nation, however, and that would be the only way that we would be able to get to the colony."

"I have heard of this place," Caleb said. "I had thought that it did not really exist, though, from the way it is talked about. And also no one seems to know where it is."

Raathe frowned hard. "I believe that I have also heard some things, although it was only snatches that I overheard and I was not able to fully understand when I missed as much as I caught of the conversation. This is where the cyborgs are fleeing to? For what purpose? To launch an attack?"

Korbin shook his head. "We have had our belly full of fighting. We only wish to be left in peace. After the disaster on Xeno-12, when we were able to escape, our leader, Reuel CO469, led an expedition to find a world that was not inhabited by humans and not easily accessible to them. We found a world that suited out needs and have colonized, are building a world for cyborgs. It is a paradise beside what we endured on Xeno-12—beside most human colonies." He shrugged. "Compared to most of what we had to deal with in the war."

"But it is for cyborgs," Raathe said pointedly. "That will not work for me. I must find a place where Tabitha will be safe ... even if I self terminate."

"They took female handlers there," Korbin pointed out. "Human females. I know of several who settled there with cyborg mates."

"You had a female handler?" Caleb asked with interest.

Korbin shook his head. "No. Our squad leader was male, but it would not have mattered. We were told that the enemy had no holdings on the planet and that we were to land and secure it as a forward position. But the Intel was faulty. The enemy began their assault before we could land and shot us to pieces. My transport did not even make it to the ground. The humans who were aboard died in the crash—including my squad leader/human handler. Most of the cyborgs were severely damaged, as well, some too damaged to continue. Some managed to drag themselves up and return fire. We retreated toward an ice ridge and discovered once there that we were trapped, cut-off from retreating further.

"So we formed a wall with the bodies of the fallen and prepared to take our last stand."

He released a snorting laugh that lacked humor. "We 'woke', most of us, on the trip down to the planet's surface, or just before we left the mother ship, so we achieved awareness just in time to endure one of the worse horrors humans could devise. The awakening only made it possible to suffer when we would not have otherwise.

"We had no leadership beyond the bastards sitting comfortably on the mother ship. We had lost most of our squad leaders and ground command before we got to the ridge.

"And then Reuel CO469 took command, ordered us to leap the ridge and carry any of the humans that were still alive. There was so much chaos by that time even the humans least damaged could not make order of the mess and they had not realized we had the capability to leap so far or it simply had not occurred to them. And we, of course, were created to obey not make decisions or suggestions, let alone issue orders.

"For saving them we were repaid with treachery. They

wanted to destroy us for going rogue and thinking for ourselves.

"Those who could escaped to join his rebel force and they took their female handlers with them if they were willing to go.

"I am not talking of rumors I have heard. I was there."

"On the world of the cyborgs?" Caleb and Raathe asked almost in sync.

He looked uncomfortable. "Briefly."

"And you know for a fact that the human women were accepted and treated well?" Raathe persisted.

"They are. Yes, I know this for a fact. They have taken cyborgs as mates. In truth, we all competed for their interest until the new council passed a law to settle the matter," he said reluctantly.

"A law? For order?"

Korbin struggled with his response. "Yes. We wanted to build a colony, to build our own world, and have what the humans have—family units. But there were very few females even counting the human women among us. To bring at least a semblance of peace, they decreed that the women must take at least three males into her household as mates. That way most, at least, had a woman even if they must share."

If Korbin had put his foot in Raathe's face he could not have been more stunned or outraged.

"You have made that up only because you want to fuck Tabitha!" Caleb growled angrily.

"Why would I make it up?" Korbin snapped angrily. "I did not *get* a woman! That is why I am out here instead of there."

"And yet you do not know how to get back there?" Raathe demanded skeptically.

"I do not! They do not allow that information to any who leave. Even those who man the outposts are not allowed to know in case they should be captured. Central command sends the coordinates to the ship's computer for the return."

Raathe was as certain as he could be that there was fault in the logic somewhere, but he was too angry to ferret it out at the moment. He needed time to consider and fit the pieces of information together. "I do not think this is something that we should discuss here—where Tabitha might stumble upon us—because I am very certain that we will have trouble convincing her to take *one* cyborg as mate! She will never agree to take three!"

Getting up decisively, he moved to the hatch that opened into the hold, opened it, and dropped through the hole.

Korbin opted to take the ladder down instead of dropping as Raathe had.

He had barely set foot on the floor, however, when Raathe leapt up, slamming his foot into his face and knocking him halfway across the hold.

Instead of following up with that preliminary, he bounded back up the ladder, slammed the door of the hold shut, and locked it.

Caleb had settled at the computer to scan the flight manual, but he swept Raathe with an uneasy glance as he straightened. "What was that about?"

Raathe narrowed his eyes at him. "Did you help him cook that up?" he growled.

"What?" Caleb asked blankly.

"The fairy tale Korbin concocted about the cyborg world so that he could fuck Tabitha?"

Caleb gobbled at him in denial. "No."

Raathe did not seem inclined to believe that, but since they heard Tabitha returning, he allowed the subject to drop … for the time being anyway.

* * * *

The faint knocking noise Tabitha had noticed a little earlier was louder when she opened the door from the cabin that led into the main area of the ship.

Consternation filled her and she rushed to the cockpit. "What's that noise?" she gasped.

Raathe turned to study her for a long moment—clearly considering his answer. "Nothing," he replied finally.

Taken aback, Tabitha gaped at him and then glanced around the cockpit. "Where's Korbin?"

"Raathe locked him in the hold," Caleb volunteered and then ducked when Raathe swung at him.

A jolt went through her. She didn't know what was more unnerving, the fact that Raathe had outright lied to her or that he'd locked Korbin in the hold. "Why?" she asked blankly.

Raathe narrowed his eyes at Caleb, daring him to answer.

Caleb glanced from him to Tabitha and shrugged.

"I believe he has gone rogue," Raathe reluctantly supplied.

Tabitha gasped, horrified. "Seriously?"

"Yes."

She frowned as doubts surfaced. "He seemed fine just a few minutes ago."

"Yes. Seemed."

Tabitha's mind went wild with speculation and then a thought surfaced and she gasped again. "You mean to say that he'd gone rogue *before* and that was why he was locked in the pen?"

Raathe seemed to think that over. "I am almost certain of it."

"I do not see how he would know," Caleb said curiously. "He had not said a word that I heard."

Raathe narrowed his eyes threateningly at Caleb.

"Well, what are we going to do? Maybe I should examine him and see if I can determine what's wrong? I do write code for the company. Maybe it's a ... virus? Or something like that?"

"I have set the main system to review his programming

and search for any anomalies."

"Oh. Poor Korbin! Well, we will have to fix the problem. I know the government would rather just pitch out anything that's the least bit defective and replace it, but I'm dead set against terminating a perfectly good cyborg when all that's needed is a little tweaking."

She knelt down on the hatch door that Korbin was beating on. "Calm down! We'll have you working at peak before you know it!"

The hammering stopped.

"Thank you, Korbin."

She got up, smiled at Raathe and Caleb and started toward the cabin before she remembered why she'd come out to start with. "What did you guys do with the stuff my father had loaded for his girlfriend?"

"I removed it," Caleb volunteered.

Dismayed, Tabitha gaped at him in angry disbelief. "You removed .... Well, damn it! I have nothing to wear and no cosmetics or hair products!"

"You do not need clothing," Raathe said. "The ship's climate is perfectly maintained."

Tabitha stared at him in bug eyed disbelief. "Walk around naked?" she gasped.

Caleb grinned at her wolfishly. "I would not mind, baby."

Raathe punched him in the mouth. "I told you not to call her baby," he growled.

Caleb punched him back, catching him on the jaw hard enough to rock his head sideways. "I do not know why I cannot! *She* does not object!"

Tabitha decided to head to the cabin. Once there, she settled on the bed to think.

Raathe had said that Korbin had gone rogue, but she was damned if it seemed to her that he had behaved any more erratically than Caleb or Raathe.

Well, except for grabbing her and humping her and

telling her he wanted to fuck.

But that had seemed almost … well, some sort of glitch—like a temporary twitch. He hadn't tried it again. She *had* caught him looking at her a couple of times and seen an expression—almost of hunger—like he needed food and she looked like food.

Of course she had found video of him watching her and Caleb together. And it seemed possible, maybe even probable, that his AI had inspired him to try it to understand it better.

After grappling with the puzzle for a while one thought stood out that was actually pretty unnerving.

What if she was wrong and everybody else was right?

What if something disturbing and very dangerous had happened to *all* of the cyborgs, not just the COs?

She'd caught Raathe lying to her—several times now. So it wasn't something she could just dismiss as some kind of programming glitch—although she supposed it couldn't really be dismissed as learned behavior.

God it would be nothing short of amazing if he *hadn't* learned to lie from her father who was a world class liar!

Kicking her shoes off, she plumped the pillows and settled more comfortably on the bed, carefully going back over every look and gesture and action of all three since she'd released them from the pens.

It wasn't easy. She'd been under duress since *before* she'd discovered them in the holding pens and the shocks, one after another, had left great gaps in her memory. When she tried to access specific events she got a whirlwind of choppy images and impressions.

She couldn't think of a single thing, though, really, that couldn't be explained away as something perfectly normal—given the circumstances, which weren't at all normal.

The three of them had been pitched into a situation that none of them had been prepared for. None of them had been designed to interact with one another and none had been programmed for the set of circumstances they'd had to deal with.

She didn't think any reasonable person would expect them to behave 'normally' and that included poor Korbin.

He was a battle model and had almost certainly just been shipped back from the front lines. There was no telling what might have happened to him on the field to alter his behavior enough that he'd been tagged as defective and returned.

She worried over it until she developed a headache and finally drowsed.

Raathe entered the room a little later, rousing her.

In more ways than one.

He was stripping when she looked up to see who'd come in.

She thought he was the most stunning man she'd ever seen, more beautiful even than Caleb—who'd been designed to please a woman.

Of course people—mostly men—held women like her in contempt for having sex with cyborgs, *preferring* sex with cyborgs to human men. Their complaint was that they were nothing but sex toys and it was 'abnormal' to crave them.

This condemnation from the sector that had been known to stick their dicks into all sorts of things that weren't human!

To her mind they simply performed better than a real man and that was reason enough for the preference. Who wanted awful sex when they were horny? It was hard to find a real man who wasn't totally focused on his pleasure to the exclusion of his partner. The cyborgs had been designed and programmed to please and they did whatever it took to please.

Beyond that, she never had to worry about whether her 'man' liked her or was just after her father's wallet. She didn't have to worry about disease or being stalked. She didn't have to worry about jealousy, cheating, or an attempt to control/dominate her—unless she requested that sort of session.

Not that she cared what any of them thought!

It was *her* life. She could live it any damned way she wanted to!

Raathe looked away as he set his clothing aside. "I will sleep during this shift and keep watch next."

Tabitha blinked at him. "Oh," she responded, shifting clumsily toward the side of the bed.

"You may sleep also if you are tired. There is room."

Tabitha hesitated. Sleep wasn't actually on her mind even though she'd had a very rough couple of days and spotty rest/sleep.

And his offer wasn't actually an invitation—not of sex anyway.

But the temptation to share the bed with him was almost too much to resist.

She shook the temptation and moved off the bed. "I think I'll go check to see what's on the menu that appeals to me for lunch."

He nodded. "I allowed Korbin out of the hold since he had calmed down."

Tabitha stopped abruptly and turned to look at him uneasily. "You think he'll be ok?"

He shrugged and settled on the bed, propping his hands behind his head and crossing his legs at his ankles. "We will see, I suppose."

Frowning, Tabitha let herself out, but she was unnerved enough to move quietly so as not to attract too much attention.

Thankfully, the door to the cockpit was closed.

She could hear a buzz of conversation that made her more than a little curious, though. She resisted the urge to eavesdrop—briefly—focusing on her voiced purpose in going to start with, but once she'd checked the menu and selected the items she wanted for the meal, she moved a little closer to the door.

She discovered she could hear their voices better, but there was still a vibration that made it impossible to make out the words.

She moved away again, staring at the com unit on the wall in the kitchen indecisively for several moments before she yielded to temptation and moved to it.

* * * *

Korbin massaged his jaw and cheek. It was still throbbing an hour since the 'discussion' he had had with Raathe.

Well, he had suggested they would have a discussion about the cyborg colony—just before he had kicked him in the face.

After he had invited him down into the hold to discuss the situation with Tabitha—specifically convincing her that they should all be her mates since she would be required to choose three.

The situation, as far as Korbin was concerned, being that *he* was the only one who had not fucked her and he had demanded to know why he was not allowed even to approach her to ask.

Again.

She had refused the first time, unfortunately, but he figured it would not hurt to ask again. She was certainly not repulsed by cyborgs or she would not have fucked Raathe and then Caleb. And she had only just spent the night fucking Caleb when he had tried to interest her. She was probably weary and would have been more receptive if he had only waited until she was rested.

Which was what he had intended to do when Raathe had diverted him with the suggestion of a discussion. He had thought that he would go back to the cabin where she was resting and ask her, very politely, if she would consider fucking him next.

He could think of no reason for Raathe to disapprove in such an ugly fashion other than a desire to jump in line ahead of him.

"I do not understand why Raathe is so brutally aggressive where Tabitha is concerned," Caleb muttered. "Tabitha did not object. In point of fact, she invited me to lie down with her and I gave her every opportunity to refuse me."

Korbin studied him thoughtfully. "She was upset."

"Yes, but I comforted her and then one thing led to another ...."

Korbin frowned, trying to figure out how that could happen.

Of course, he had watched when he had discovered that he could, but they were already fucking by that time. He did not get the chance to see how it came to that point.

"I would almost be tempted to throw him out of the airlock if not for the fact that I am completely convinced Tabitha would not forgive me for that."

Korbin nodded. "She seems very attached to him. I am damned if I know why. He is a foul tempered bastard and quick with his fists."

They fell silent, considering that for a few minutes.

When Caleb emerged from his thoughts, he studied Korbin speculatively. "I was not programmed to fight as Raathe was. I have no programming beyond human sexuality, and the social skills necessary for successful flirtation and intimacy. And I have found that it is very difficult to use AI to learn the moves in real time. Raathe moves far too fast and he never does the same thing twice. It is very difficult to know what to do when he is never predictable."

Korbin frowned. "His fight program is not the same as mine either. There is no discipline. He called it street fighting, but I do not even have that in my data banks. The hand to hand combat is somewhat recognizable ...."

Caleb's enthusiasm nosedived, but there was no getting around the fact that Korbin fared far better in a contest against Raathe than he did. "I was wondering if you would consider allowing me to access your combat programming? Then I would be better prepared the next time I fall afoul of Raathe."

Korbin studied him thoughtfully. "I would certainly consider that if you would allow me to access your programming on human sexuality and social skills. I do not have those so I am handicapped in romancing Tabitha. I want to fuck with her and make a baby. Or perhaps more than one. I would like to make a family unit."

Caleb instantly put on brakes. "I thought we were talking about fucking. Where did making babies come in to the discussion?"

Korbin looked at him curiously. "I just put that into the discussion. Fucking is making a baby, yes? My computer says that it is the vernacular for copulation—which is the act of reproducing."

"For humans. We are not human."

Korbin glared at him. "*I* can make a baby," he growled, daring Caleb to disagree. "Mayhap *you* are not capable, but I am."

"What makes you think that *you* can? And that I cannot?" Caleb demanded angrily.

* * * *

Tabitha was so stunned she almost forgot to turn off the com unit. She was already headed to the master cabin, however, before she heard the first salvo of the fight she'd heard brewing between Caleb and Korbin. Dashing inside, she kicked her shoes off, stripped off her trousers and dove under the covers with Raathe in her shirt and panties in an effort to pretend she'd been sleeping the entire time, huddling as close to his back as she could get.

He roused and turned over.

Tabitha squeezed her eyes more tightly shut, struggling to think of how she could believably feign sleep.

"What are you doing?"

She opened her eyes to look at him. "You said I could sleep here if I was tired."

He frowned. "You are very tense," he said after a long pause.

"Yes. I am. That's why I haven't been able to sleep ... much. Because I've been very tense."

"You are also cold," Raathe murmured when he had stroked a hand lightly down her arm. "And you are shaking."

She couldn't think of a response for that.

Settling again, Raathe pulled her close against his length and wrapped his arms around her, slowly stroking her back.

As if that was going to help her relax when he was buck ass naked and she was wedged against his cock! It felt like a fire iron on her belly.

On the other hand, he *was* generating a good bit of heat.

Chapter Eleven

"You are not tired," Raathe said after a handful of

moments. "You are afraid. What has frightened you, Tabby?"

Tabby debated whether to tell him what she'd overheard or not.

It was bound to throw him into a rage and then he'd stop doing what he was doing and it felt really nice. "Could we … just not talk about it now? This feels … really good."

He paused. "What does?"

He sounded genuinely puzzled and she smiled against his chest. "If I tell you, will you stop?"

He pulled a little away so that he could study her expression. Finally, he lifted a hand to her cheek and brushed away a strand of hair. "You do not want me to stop?" he asked pensively.

She held his gaze and shook her head slowly.

"Because I am a cyborg—not a real man—and there are no consequences because of that?"

She swallowed with an effort, wondering how much he knew about that conversation that had disturbed her so much.

She realized abruptly that that was probably the reason he had fought with Korbin and locked him in the hold.

Well, Korbin had not specifically said so, but she thought from what she'd heard that it must have been something to that effect.

He rolled over her when she didn't answer, pressing her into the mattress with his body despite the fact that he was still supporting most of his weight with his arms and legs.

She welcomed the feel of his weight on her, though, realizing that it felt comforting, protective, not threatening in any way even though, in a very real sense, he had put her into the position of submissive to his domination.

Because it was Raathe.

He captured her arms, dragging them above her head and manacling both wrists with one hand while he used the other to pluck the buttons from her shirt and spread it wide.

He cupped the breast he could reach gently, massaged it. The nipple stood straight up and tightened, trembled with each heartbeat. He studied it for a long moment and then met her gaze as he slowly leaned down.

She watched him as he transferred his focus to the target—her nipple—unconsciously holding her breath as she watched his lips part and then felt them tighten around the hard tip. He plucked at it a couple of times, until it began to throb painfully with the blood engorging it. The stroke of his faintly rough tongue felt as if it had knocked the breath from her. And then she felt him curl his tongue around her nipple and the pull of his mouth.

She closed her eyes, felt them roll back in her head as the scorching heat of his mouth transferred to that delicate tip and formed a fiery trail through her body to her womb. That organ contracted—hard—forcing liquid want into her channel. With each pull of his mouth, the heat and moisture and tension built.

She arched her back in offering, panting for breath, feeling drunk and dizzy and … lost. Lost to herself. Focused so completely on him that she felt every scalding breath he exhaled as it made its way inside of her and claimed her.

She was writhing beneath him with the fever of desperate need when he ceased to torment her nipple and lifted his head to study her face.

She opened her eyes with an effort and met his gaze.

His eyes were tumultuous, his face like stone.

Her entire body seemed to clench at that look.

"Raathe?" she whispered doubtfully.

He covered her mouth with his then, kissed her deeply, stroking his tongue along hers, sucking on it when he'd coaxed it into his mouth.

She was beyond ready for his claiming when he broke the kiss and stripped her panties from her. She had gasped for air until she thought she might pass out.

Instead of positioning himself to claim her, however, he leaned down and found her neglected breast when he shifted his position, capturing that peak in his mouth and tormenting it as he had the first until she was nearing blackout from struggling to suck air into her collapsed lungs.

It was a relief when he finally released the throbbing nub.

For a handful of seconds.

He let go of her wrists and planted a huge hand on each of her knees, pushing them up until her thighs were against her body and then spreading them wide.

He stared down at her then—as if contemplating his next move—and then, just when she thought he meant to give her what she'd been whimpering for, he shifted downward on the bed and planted his mouth over her sex, capturing the throbbing nub of her clit as he had each of her nipples.

She felt like the top of her skull flew off with the first suck and her brains spilled out. She gasped and fought him mindlessly, fought the intensity of the keen sensations that tore through her. It was too powerful to bear.

He didn't give her a choice. He wove his arms through her legs and captured her wrists so that she was pinned and completely at his mercy and then he mercilessly sucked her clit until her body exploded with rapture so intense she felt like she would die from it. Her gasps became harsher, became screams. Her mind turned to mush. There was nothing left but the fierce palpitations pounding through her.

Her heart was pounding so loudly in her ears, her wits so scattered, that she hardly knew when he finally stopped until he released her, allowing her accordion pleated body to relax.

He crawled over her then, settling his slender hips in the cradle of her shaking, splayed thighs and pressing the head of his cock against her throbbing sex.

She groaned, but she wasn't able to actually vocalize her dismay that he wasn't done with her yet, that he expected to wring more from her. She finally managed to say his name in a hoarse whisper.

She supposed he interpreted that to mean she was ready. He curled his arms around her to hold her in place while he pried the mouth of her sex open and embedded the head of his cock. He paused then, as if to catch his breath, and then abruptly changed positions altogether. Going up on his knees, he carried her with him, using her weight to help in the effort to claim her taut, quaking channel.

The claiming was a trial for both of them for all that, a struggle to merge flesh to flesh that was still clenched with the convulsions of the massive climax she'd just had.

Despite that, without reason or logic to Tabitha's mind, her body leapt up to the quivering verge of another release. And she was nearly weeping with desperation by the time he managed to overpower the resistance of her flesh and drive deep.

Speared by the blunt object, her womb cramped, but it had no appreciable effect that she could tell in slowing her reach toward another culmination. Almost as soon as Raathe began to jog her up and down his cock, sinking so deeply each time there was almost as much pain as pleasure, her body gathered itself and jumped.

That climax was harder than the first—harder because it seemed to encompass her entire being, to leave no part of her untouched, quaking through every muscle and sinew and cell until it felt as if it would tear her apart.

It had reached fever pitch when Raathe uttered a deep throated grunt, stilled for a handful of seconds, and then tightened his grip on her and pumped into her in short, deep thrusts while his body shook so hard it shook hers.

There was something about that circumstance that just didn't seem entirely right, especially when it was followed by a gush of heated fluids that bathed her womb.

She was too far gone to analyze it, she decided as she felt herself drifting, sinking toward oblivion as the last of the convulsions, thankfully, died off, leaving her feeling as substantial as a jelly fish. She'd think about that later and figure out why it seemed 'wrong'.

At the moment she was just grateful to be supported by Raathe's strong arms.

He shifted his hold on her, cupping a hand on the back of her head and then stroking a trail of kisses up her throat. Then he moved with great care to remain connected and settled the two of them on the mattress.

Tabitha ended up sprawled limply on top of him. She hadn't actually been tired or sleepy when she'd headed to the cabin. She'd fled instinctively to Raathe—who had always been her safe harbor no matter how frightening the world was. Now she was beyond tired. She was completely bereft of energy, stripped of even an ounce of stress.

She was out almost the instant they settled.

It dawned on her as she drifted away, though, that Raathe hadn't simulated a climax as most newer models of pleasure droids were programmed to do—because he wasn't a pleasure model.

Caleb *might* have been upgraded to simulate orgasm— but she couldn't think of a single, rational explanation for why Raathe would have been.

* * * *

Raathe dreamed.

It felt like a memory and yet there was none of the pain he had come to associate with the efforts of his brain to pull those biological recordings into the light.

He was naked and the girl that he was with was also naked and they lay entwined—girl because she was too young to be a woman and he was young also, too young to be a man. Darkness enveloped them. He knew they had just had sex even though there were no memories of it. In the distance he heard the faint sounds of laughter, music … a party?

Then he rolled onto his side, away from the girl, and found himself face to face with a grisly corpse. And he knew he was lying on a battlefield, surrounded by the dead and dying.

He sucked in a sharp breath and woke with a jerk that roused Tabitha.

She lifted her head and stared at him bleary eyed for a long moment, as if trying to recall where she was.

And then she smiled at him and he felt it in a stirring of warmth in his chest, a light airiness that chased the chill away from the horrific image that had snatched him from sleep.

And she sighed and closed her eyes again. "That was … something else," she murmured, snuggling her cheek against his chest. "Thank you, Raathe."

He struggled not to interpret that as a pat on the head for a 'good dog', but, unfortunately, he could not dismiss it as he wanted to. It was all he had ever known by way of appreciation from the humans that surrounded him—and there had been little enough of that.

"Do you say that to your human lovers?" he asked, trying to keep his voice even.

Her lips curled into a secret smile. "No. Well, only ever had a couple—but no."

"I did not think so."

She opened her eyes and studied him. "Because they aren't even half as good."

He shook his head, carefully pushed her onto the mattress, and sat up. Moving to the side of the bed, he sat on the edge, holding his head in his hands and absently massaging the dull throb there.

He stiffened when he felt Tabitha move up behind him. She came up on her knees, pressing her breasts to his back as she leaned against him and cupped her hands around his head. "Where does it hurt?"

"It does not. I cannot feel pain."

She knew that both statements were lies. She'd heard him telling Korbin it hurt. She'd seen him massaging it.

It seemed grossly unfair for him to feel any sort of pain, but maybe it was just a malfunction of some kind?

She massaged his head anyway and then his shoulders. He wasn't entirely a machine even though, legally, he was considered a machine. He was part biological and it was not only possible he was feeling pain, but she thought it was also possible the pressure could help.

He seemed to relax. "Why were you frightened when you came in?"

Tabitha tensed, wondering if she should say anything at all. The ship was not all that big and they had a very long voyage ahead of them. It seemed unwise to start something that would create dissension.

"I overheard Korbin and Caleb," she admitted finally when it occurred to her that he was very likely to go pound on them until they told him regardless of what she did or didn't do at this point.

He twisted away from her and turned to search her face with his gaze. "They did not hear your approach?" he asked doubtfully.

Tabitha felt her face redden. She chewed her lip, reluctant to admit she'd been eavesdropping. But then, he was never going to believe they spoke openly about those things or that she'd managed to sneak up on them. "I heard the murmur of voices and I used the com unit in the kitchen to listen."

He frowned, clearly disapproving. "Your father did not teach you the error of such things, I see."

Guilt flooded her and anger followed. And her brains went right out the window! "Well it seemed ... like it might be a threat of some kind, and when I listened I heard …." She plowed to a stop as it dawned on her that Raathe had shown a great deal of animosity toward Caleb already and that it would probably be a bad idea to tell him Caleb had been talking about pitching him out of the airlock.

And she knew he hadn't really meant it.

And he couldn't overpower Raathe even if he had.

But Raathe was liable to try to pitch Caleb out if he knew about the supposed threat.

"You heard?" he prompted.

"Crazy stuff! Korbin was talking about making a baby with me! I really think you might be right about him—that he went rogue. I mean, he doesn't *seem* dangerous. He's very respectful, but he's just ... well he's a huge ... uh ... and he was programmed as a soldier." Stupid! Stupid! Stupid! He was no bigger than Raathe and Raathe might well take exception to the suggestion that he was a monster.

Raathe's gaze went to her belly when she mentioned making a baby and stayed there. "He cannot make a baby with you," he growled, meeting her gaze after a long moment. "I have done that already."

The only reason Tabitha's jaw didn't hit the floor was because she was kneeling on the bed. She blinked at him—rapidly—trying to process what he'd said and figure out how she could have thought he'd said what she thought he had. "What?"

"I have made a baby on you," he repeated, slowly, as if to a halfwit.

She went back to blinking, trying to think what the safest course of action might be.

Because clearly Raathe was *also* insane!

She struggled to keep from bursting into tears, wondering if it was connected to the pain he had been experiencing in his brain.

A terminal defect! And she hadn't had a clue!

Her poor, darling Raathe! She swallowed with great difficulty against the hard knot of emotion that formed in her throat.

She decided he looked too belligerent at the moment to attempt to reason with him. "Oh! Well, that's a relief!"

He studied her skeptically. "You are relieved that you are carrying my offspring?"

She smiled at him woodenly. She'd certainly flubbed that, but she couldn't think of anything to do except try to smooth the stupid response and make it sound more believable. "I always meant to have a baby—uh one day. Remember? I did mention that was why I'd gotten a two bedroom," she said cheerfully instead of pointing out that she couldn't possibly be carrying his child because he could not make one and that he wouldn't know even if she *was* pregnant. Which was impossible since she hadn't been exposed to real semen in more than a year.

His gaze moved over her face. "You cannot accept that I am as 'real' as you are? That I am a sentient being—even if I am not a human being?"

Dismay flickered through Tabitha. "Don't look at me like that! You know that I've always …." She swallowed with an effort.

"Always what, Tabby? Considered me your favorite pet?"

She shook her head at him, too dismayed to consider protecting herself. "You are a fool if you believe that! I never questioned whether you were human or not … because it never mattered to me. You are what you are and I love you just the way you are and always have."

Raathe met her gaze with a look of intensity she found hard to maintain and finally shook his head, realizing he had no real choice. Even if he hated this place Korbin had spoken of—hated that he might actually have no choice about whether to share Tabitha or not, he realized it was something they must do to have any kind of life at all. They could settle where they might find a welcome, or they could run until they were caught. "Yes. Humans love their possessions. I know this. And that you have a great deal of affection for this CHS300 because of that, but I am not what I was, Tabby. I am not a thing anymore, a tool, a mindless machine awaiting instructions—with no feelings, without emotion or a true understanding of what being alive means. I have achieved awareness, identity, and a desire to find my place in the universe. I am a living being. I want what all living things do. I want ... a real family ... want to have a child."

Tabitha felt an overwhelming urge to hold him, but he pulled away and stood when she reached for him.

"This may not be what you want, Tabby, but I cannot leave you to the machinations of your father or to pay for his crimes ... and I can no longer stay in the human world. I have to find my place, my freedom. And the only way that I can carry out my obligation to keep you safe is to take you with me."

She was still gaping at the place where he'd been when he stalked out of the cabin, wondering what he meant by that.

Was he saying she was nothing more to him than an obligation? That he didn't really care about her? He was just doing what he had been designed and programmed to do?

Was he saying that he had gone rogue, too?

She certainly wasn't going to argue about paying for her father's crimes—whatever those were—but what had he meant by 'it might not be what she wanted'?

She had believed they were headed to her father's safe house.

Was she a prisoner?

Had she been kidnapped by the very man she had thought, trusted, would keep her safe?

Chapter Twelve

It took an effort for Raathe to reign in his anger when he reached the cockpit.

Caleb and Korbin were panting for breath—a clear indication that they had only broken off fighting to catch their second wind to start again.

The cockpit was a disaster area.

"What the fuck?" he growled. "Do you both have a death wish? If you want to fight, by all means help yourself, but use the hold where you will do less damage. And are not as likely to wreck the ship."

Korbin looked sheepish. "I had not thought …."

"*That* is obvious! Tabitha overheard the conversation, by the way. She was … frightened."

Korbin's eyes widened and he glanced at Caleb, but then his dark brows descended and he looked puzzled. "I cannot recall that I said anything that would have frightened her."

"Mayhap because you are a moron and have no clue of what might frighten a human woman?"

Korbin had clearly mixed feelings over that statement. "And how am I supposed to have a clue of what would frighten a human woman?" he growled. "Tabitha is the only human woman I have been near who was not also a soldier. And that asshole will not share his programming! What part frightened her?"

Raathe settled in the pilot's seat. "The part where you wanted to fuck her and make a baby," he said coolly.

Korbin was more confused, not less. "That is what the mating is about, is it not? To produce offspring? And that cannot be done without the fucking."

"More or less—as I understand the process," Raathe said dryly. "I have not had much opportunity to observe and learn that myself. Langston's mate was dead before I was purchased and he seemed content not to take a mate again.

"And Tabitha has taken no mate."

Caleb studied him thoughtfully. "She has not said that she will accept you as a mate? She seems willing enough to me."

The question threw Raathe for a loop. It had not occurred to him to ask her. He struggled with the urge to ask Caleb if that was how it was done—one simply asked—but he did not want Caleb to know it had not occurred to him and that he had not done so. "She has not yet come to terms with the fact that we are not merely machines anymore. She must accept that before she can accept me—or anyone—as a mate. There can be no contract—verbal or otherwise—with a machine.

"And, in any case, I do not perfectly understand this business of taking multiple partners into the family units."

"Naturally, I know nothing about family units, but it is not particularly difficult to have sex with more than one," Caleb offered. "I have done so. Of course that was me with two females, but it would not take a great deal of inventiveness to switch that to two males and one female and it could be very gratifying for all."

Korbin and Raathe both stared at him in fascination for a long moment before they dismissed his input.

Korbin shrugged. "You may be certain no one was fully satisfied with the solution, but, in truth, there was nothing else that had any chance of working and satisfying the majority. There are human societies, I am told, where this is typical—and for the same reason—a severe imbalance between the numbers of males and females. It is legalized by contract and the members of the family group must work out their differences if they want peace in their homes." He shrugged. "It is a solution based upon the facts that cannot be changed."

The facts being there were three or four times as many males as females.

That resurrected the disturbing thoughts he'd had earlier, and the prospects of a grim future if they ignored reason and logic and allowed emotion to rule, if they chose to fly in the face of logic and go their own way.

And if he had impregnated Tabitha as he believed, then that would be an even harder life for a child.

He could not leave her with her own kind even though he had considered that possibility. He would have to stay and protect her and the child—assuming he had made one—and that would endanger them.

She would pay for harboring a cyborg if/when they were caught.

And the child would most likely be put down as he would be.

In the end, he decided there really were no options even though it seemed as if they had a choice.

He would take her to the cyborg nation so that she and their child would be safe.

But that opened other unpalatable possibilities.

He did not particularly like the notion of sharing his woman with Caleb and Korbin, but the alternative appealed even less. Better the devils he knew than two that were unknown entities.

And, truth be told, he was not at all certain that Tabitha considered him her man—or would. He knew that she had a fondness for him, but he also knew that it could not be the affection of a woman for a man because he did not believe that she had ever thought of him that way, regardless of what she said to the contrary.

He could not tell that she thought of him or looked upon him any differently than she ever had.

He had never been at her command, but that had not stopped her from issuing commands.

He frowned, thinking that over and decided that he was wrong. There had been a subtle shift—so subtle that he had not even noticed until he had considered it.

He got up abruptly. "You two must finish your match in the hold—and try not to do any serious damage!"

Tabitha was standing by the com unit wearing her guilty look and nothing else when he entered the master cabin again.

He glanced from her to the com unit and back again, and then strode to her and scooped her up. "Clearly this is an invitation," he murmured, heading for the bed.

He dropped her there and stripped his uniform off.

Tabitha gaped at him, but the moment he began to strip, she retreated to the other side of the bunk and tried to get off.

He dove across the bed and dragged her back, beneath him, caging her with his arms and legs.

She stared up at him bug-eyed. "What are you doing?"

He tilted his head and began to nibble her cheek and jaw. "Convincing you," he murmured.

He felt the tension ease from her. "Of what?"

He made his way down to her breasts and plucked at first one nipple and then the other. "What do you think?"

She gasped. "About what?" she asked vaguely.

He lifted his head. Stroking one hand down her length until he could grasp her thigh, he lifted it and rolled into the space he'd made between her thighs, finding the mouth of her sex with the head of his cock unerringly. "He knows his way now," he murmured, watching her face as he sawed slowly and shallowly, inching his way inside of her.

The expression on her face set his heart to hammering in his chest as if he had run a mile. His lungs labored. He slipped his arms around her, curling his hips to probe deeper and deeper until he had seated himself balls deep.

She was panting for breath.

She groaned as he lifted his hips and dragged his cock along her channel.

"Do you see me, baby?" he murmured hoarsely.

She opened her eyes with an effort and stared at his face dizzily, her eyes so glazed he saw passion but little comprehension of the question. "Raathe," she whispered as her vision focused.

"I have always been your man."

"I know."

"I want you to be my woman—to bear my child."

Something flickered in her eyes. "I've always been your woman–even when you didn't know it."

Raathe stared at her, struggling against the tightness in his chest, struggling with his doubts, but he lost the battle with his desire in that moment. Plunging deeply inside of her again, he set an almost frenzied pace, thrusting and retreating until he felt his body tighten and then disgorge his semen into her in hard, gut wrenching convulsions.

He was not so lost to the world, though, that he did not feel the response of her body to his, feel the quakes that went through her or miss her whispered confession.

"I love you, Raathe. I always did."

It was unfortunate that he could not simply accept that as fact. He would have been far happier if he had not suspected that she was only saying what she knew he desperately wanted to hear, but he could not recall that she had ever behaved as if she was even as fond of him as she was her favorite purse and shoes.

He was not ready to give up, however. He was certain that he could convince her and he intended to before he allowed either Caleb or Korbin to attempt to convince her to accept them!

* * * *

"Gods damn it! He has gone back to fuck more!" Caleb growled. "And I have only fucked her twice in my entire existence!"

Korbin frowned. "How do you know?"

"It was the cock tenting his trousers that gave it away."

Korbin shoved himself to his feet. "That is … well I do not know what that is, but it pisses me off! I have not fucked at all!"

Caleb shot out of his chair and shoved his face into

Korbin's. "I have told you, gods damn it, it is not fucking when it is a lady!"

Korbin grabbed him by the throat and lifted him clear of the floor. "You called it fucking just now! And you did not say what it was called when it was a lady, gods damn it! And I do not see that it matters what it is called when it is the same damned thing! I want to stick my cock in her and jog her up and down until I ejaculate!"

Caleb punched him in the belly several times, trying to convince Korbin to let go of his throat, but Korbin seemed unfazed. Instead of letting him go, he dragged him to the hatch to the hold, opened it and then shoved him in. Before Caleb could scramble to his feet, Korbin had slammed the door shut and latched it.

Caleb considered trying to beat the door down but since Korbin had not seemed to have much luck with that he decided it was a waste of energy.

And he was already weary from allowing Korbin to mop the cockpit with him.

He decided to rest to conserve the energy he had since it seemed doubtful that he would get food any time soon.

Especially since Raathe had gone back to the cabin to discuss mating with Tabitha. It seemed likely they would discuss it much of the day period and he would be lucky to be fed at all before the next day cycle.

It turned out that he had miscalculated.

Several day cycles passed before Tabitha managed to escape while Raathe was bathing.

Fortunately, Korbin decided to let him out toward the end of that day cycle and they shared a meal in the kitchen while Raathe and Tabitha supposedly shared one in the master cabin.

* * * *

Tabitha faked sleep until Raathe disappeared into the private bath and then bounded out of bed, grabbed a shirt to cover her nakedness, and fled the master cabin. Her thighs screamed at the activity, but she ignored it and the semen trail down her thighs, ducking into the second bath for a quick clean up.

As she'd hoped, there was a guest robe hanging in the bath. She snatched it down and dove into it and then headed into the kitchen.

Caleb was at the table wolfing down a plate of steak and eggs when she arrived, but he halted with his fork halfway to his mouth when he spied her.

Smiling at him uneasily, she flicked a quick look at Korbin and then dove into the booth seat beside Caleb.

"I don't suppose you would fix me a plate like that?" she asked Korbin when she discovered he was staring at her.

He looked down at the plate in his hand and then strode to the table and set it down in front of her.

"Thanks, Korbin!" she said gratefully, digging into the food immediately.

She was starving—absolutely starving to death!

Raathe had been fucking her for three days straight and no amount of food could sustain that much expenditure of energy!

She was sore and she was exhausted and she was starving!

Not that she had any other complaints! She didn't actually *need* that much sex, but it was still fabulous sex!

She didn't have a *clue* of why Raathe had suddenly set out to fuck her to death, but he had worked very hard to please—not just focused on his own needs.

Which she supposed should have been questionable.

He was a cyborg. He shouldn't have needs.

He shouldn't have felt desire—shouldn't have said or done a lot of things.

And he wouldn't have been able to if he was nothing more than a cyborg.

She was finding it nearly impossible to continue to maintain that that was all he was—just a cyborg that was somewhat defective.

Well, she wasn't actually trying to convince herself anymore.

The truth was she *wanted* to believe he had been transformed into a real man.

It had been her secret fantasy almost from the moment she was old enough to think about boys and mating in the same thought stream.

Except she just never could really get 'in' to the boys.

They fell too far short of Raathe in every way.

He was her ideal. She'd spent almost as much time fantasizing about finding a man that could stand up to the comparison as she had fantasizing that she didn't need to. She had Raathe. He was all she really needed.

Although, of course, he wasn't.

There had been a very drastic change in him since she had seen him last, though.

He *behaved* like a real man.

It seemed unbelievable to her that he could have made the leap from artificial to real, but it was hard to dismiss what her senses told her.

She was inclined to allow him to convince her and be done with it.

Real or not, she could do far worse than accept Raathe as her man.

Of course, regardless of what he thought, she was pretty sure that meant giving up her dreams of being a mother one day, but she'd very likely lost that opportunity anyway.

She was a fugitive now.

If she tried to straighten that out, she might end in jail and she would be too old to have a natural child by the time she got out, she was sure. She might put up eggs for that day and manage a late life pregnancy—or not.

But she might actually manage something like that and keep her freedom if she stayed with Raathe.

And who was she kidding? She knew she couldn't bear

it if he left her and she never saw him again. She would spend the rest of her life wondering what had become of him, if he'd overcome the issue with his brain or died from it.

No. As she had said, she was his and always had been. She just needed to convince him not to try to convince *her* anymore.

As if that thought had produced him, he stepped through the door of the master cabin at just that moment, wearing only a towel around his waist.

Without any appearance of running, Korbin crossed the kitchen briskly with his plate and squeezed into the booth on Tabitha's other side, sandwiching her between him and Caleb.

Tabitha dragged her gaze from Raathe and glanced at the men on either side of her and then focused on her plate of food, ignoring Raathe until he stopped staring a hole through her and returned to the cabin.

Breathing a sigh of relief, Tabitha set her fork down and took a drink from Caleb's cup.

He watched the cup as she lifted it and then set it down. "You are thirsty?"

"Completely dehydrated," Tabitha agreed before she considered her words and then blushed at what that seemed to imply.

Korbin studied the door to the master cabin and finally leapt up and strode to the refrigeration unit to grab juice.

Raathe almost beat him back to the table, but he was closer and faster.

He narrowed his eyes at Korbin as Korbin poured Tabitha a drink, pretending he was completely oblivious.

After hesitating for a few minutes, Raathe moved to the food processor and punched in an order for food. Leaning back against the counter, he folded his arms while he waited. "Tabby has agreed to be my woman," he said challengingly.

Korbin and Caleb both lifted their heads to stare at him at that and then transferred their attention to Tabitha. She felt her face heat at the inspection. "Yep! Sure did! Sooo … that's settled. I'm Raathe's woman. We're mated! Completely!"

"You must choose two more," Korbin said after a long moment. "It is the law of the cyborg nation. I would like to offer myself as your man, as well."

Tabitha's jaw dropped with dismay. She tried, but that was all she could pull out at the moment. She'd had more sex in the past couple of days than in all of her life prior. She had climaxed until she thought she was going to have a heart attack and die. She could barely summon enough moisture to spit, and she was beyond exhausted. And that didn't even begin to describe how sore she was—everywhere—but most especially her hole. "Oh my god! Seriously? I do? I must?" She frowned. "What is the Cyborg Nation? Are we going there then? I thought we were going to my father's compound on Destiny?"

"We *are* going to destiny," Raathe agreed. "We are going there to try to contact the cyborgs who can tell us the way."

Chapter Thirteen

Tabitha had never had a harder time looking delighted.

Of all the scenarios that had played through her mind, though, that one hadn't ... and for a very good reason.

She wasn't convinced that being stuck in the middle of thousands of rogue cyborgs was going to be any more beneficial to her health than spending time in a human prison. She would still be surrounded by very dangerous people, but she might live to get out of the prison.

To avoid any possibility of going to prison, she first had to accept three cyborgs as mates.

Not that she wasn't fond of all of them. She was more than fond of Raathe, actually, and felt almost as attached to Caleb--in a very different way. And she couldn't deny that Korbin had been growing on her. It was hard not to feel a growing attachment to a man that was so very beautiful and still seemed to think *she* was.

No—it wasn't a lack of feelings for them that led to the dread. It was the enthusiasm of the group to demonstrate their affection for her. Raathe had amazed and delighted her—almost to the point of expiring, and that was the hitch. She didn't think she was up to keeping up with one cyborg—if that cyborg was Raathe—let alone three.

Because they seemed very unaware of the frailty of the human condition despite their programming on that subject.

She supposed she was going to find out whether she could or not—regardless. They all seemed pretty dead set on convincing her that they were a perfect match for her and they had barely begun what promised to be a very, very long voyage.

She was pretty sure she wasn't going to be able to placate them and hold them off that long.

Plan B, she supposed, would be to lull them into a sense of triumph with sex.

Well, she just wasn't up to that at the moment.

So maybe Plan C could be agreeing with them now, paying later, and then escaping much later if she still thought that was better than heading into no man's land-- literally?

It might work.

She couldn't think of any other options. "Ok, then," she said with forced cheer. "I guess that means you guys and I–all three of you—are a … uh … family unit now! I don't see that we need to consummate the deal—right this moment, I mean. That can wait, right?"

She couldn't help but notice that none of the three looked happy or convinced that she was sincere.

Which unnerved her just a little since she wasn't sincere but hadn't expected them to see right through her ploy.

"Just like that?" Raathe demanded, clearly outraged.

She decided that warranted a counterattack—the best defense was a good offense! "What do you mean 'just like that'? I can't make up my mind without being doubted? Or are you suggesting that you didn't enjoy … uh … all that time you spent convincing me?"

He came within a hair's breadth of pointing out how hard he had worked to convince her when they had done nothing at all to earn her trust or her affection. It occurred to him, though, that he could not think of any way to express those sentiments that would not sound as if he resented that *he* had spent three days convincing her.

And that was certainly not the case.

It had been beyond anything he had expected even after their first time together.

However, it was grossly unfair, as far as he was concerned, that she could accept them under so short an acquaintance.

Of course, the truth was that he had been nothing more than a machine before he had awakened and he supposed that time did not really count. And then there was the fact that he did not see her at all until he had been in the pen awaiting destruction.

He supposed, given those facts, that he could not claim a great deal of prior association with her.

He still felt that the situation was not even or just and that it was not stacked in his favor when it should have been by rights.

It did occur to him after a few moments, though, that he should be gloating not pissed. He had spent three nights with her wringing pleasure from her, receiving pleasure.

Now she was saying she would accept Caleb and Korbin without that.

Good, he thought. They will not have what I have!

Unfortunately for the sake of peace, both Caleb and Korbin realized they'd been gypped. Almost the moment Tabitha had eaten and headed back to the master cabin to sleep, their resentment spilled over into a heated argument and then, when they retired to the hold to keep the noise level from disturbing Tabitha's sleep, an all out battle.

It took them all of two hours to deplete their energy levels to a point where they were forced to sit down and rest and consider whether they had enough energy to continue. But it wasn't really a rational decision. Almost as soon as they settled to catch their breath, the argument, the sense of mistreatment and favoritism boiled over again and they staggered up and went several more rounds. They only stopped when they reached the point where it took more strength than they had to lift their fists again. Then they settled to catch their breaths and try to gather enough energy to climb out of the hold before they expired.

"I do not even know why you are here," Korbin growled at Caleb resentfully. "You have fucked her twice."

Caleb glared back at him but decided there was no sense in provoking him by pointing out that he and Tabitha had made love several times during the course of that night they'd spent together, that in actual fact they had made love *most* of the night that first time they were together. So, technically, he had had sex with Tabitha many times—but only on two separate occasions. "The first should not count," he said after a prolonged moment. "I had not awakened then. I gave as much joy as I knew how, but the only enjoyment I got from it was that I gave her pleasure."

Raathe felt the hate rise that he always felt when Caleb reminded him of that time, but he discovered he was down to minimum reserves in regards to energy and decided he would have to beat the fuck out of him later. "You should not have touched her at all," he growled.

Caleb looked at him for a long moment. "You had the option of ignoring the orders of your master?" he asked finally.

That question pierced Raathe's anger and deflated it fairly effectively.

"Because I was not able to do that. In fact, it was only after I awakened that it occurred to me that I wished to—and since I was not free even then, the only way I could preserve my life was to try to convince everyone that I had not changed. So I still did just as I was told."

"At least you got to fuck," Korbin snapped. "I have done nothing but kill and dodge bullets in my entire existence."

"Yes. I was designed and programmed for it," Caleb said with some bitterness. "I was sold first to a lovely, somewhat demented woman, whose pleasure was to inflict as much damage as possible to relieve her stress. Sometimes she wanted me to beat her instead and then was angry because my inhibitors made it impossible for me to comply. Then she had a crank modify my programming so that I was able to perform sexual sadism, but it still deeply disturbed my logic circuits and I kept breaking down. Then she sold me to the brothel. I was an older model by then and had been modified so they decided it would be better to use me for clients looking for BDSM and so that is almost exclusively what I did until the night that Tabitha decided she wanted me.

"I could not have refused if I had wanted to and, even if I had had that capability then, I would not have wanted to. She was … untainted by strange cravings, not jaded from having all the sex she wanted any time she wanted. She was sweet and clean and wholesome and good—things most of the women who used me had very little familiarity with.

"I think she was the only thing that kept me sane."

Raathe and Korbin both stared at him uncomfortably for several moments and then struggled to their feet with an effort and climbed out of the hold, leaving Caleb to wonder if he should have said anything at all.

He had felt nothing since his awakening but shame for all the things he remembered that he had done—because he was ordered to. If he had thought he could erase all of it and leave his memories of Tabitha untouched, he would have. But he thought that it was worth remembering the bad to keep that.

He thought at first that he regretted sharing his shame but after thinking it over for a while he realized that he felt less shame than he had, and less disturbed by his memories. And then, too, it occurred to him that—if it was true that they were all Tabitha's mates, then they were brothers in a sense.

They hadn't seemed inclined to torment him about it.

* * * *

Tabitha hadn't actually expected the guys to take it to heart when she'd told them there was no need to consummate their agreement, but weeks passed and no one took the initiative. For the better part of a month they did nothing to entertain themselves but play card and board games, watch the broadcasts they picked up whenever they were close enough to a source to do so, watch videos when they weren't, read books, listen to music, eat and sleep.

The deadly boredom of a prolonged space trip aside,

Tabitha was surrounded by three men she was very attracted to, had been reintroduced to the pleasures of the flesh with a dedication and frequency to taking her to rapturous heights that had gotten her addicted to the sport—at least where they were concerned—and had been coerced into accepting them as mates.

She was horny, damn it!

Unfortunately, she was not comfortable with the idea of initiating sex, and she was inexperienced in seduction.

Hints went right over their heads.

Broad hints, too.

The three of them would look at her as if they could eat her alive, but they were clearly waiting to be invited to the table, damn it!

Finally, when Tabitha had decided she was just going to have to forget about spontaneity and demand service, Caleb nerved himself to brave the possibility of rejection and 'sneaked' into her bed one night when he thought she was sleeping.

She discovered she really enjoyed the game. Pretending to be asleep encouraged him to try harder to get a response out of her and made for a lot of wow. It didn't tax her acting skills at all. She simply laid on the bed like a dead thing and enjoyed, 'coming around' at the crucial moment and enjoying an explosive climax.

She did feel a little guilty that she hadn't made any effort to give, but he *had* woke her up and she'd *still* let him have sex and not tried to bash his head in, and as far as she could see he enjoyed it as much as she did.

So much in fact, that he was ready to go again very shortly afterward—just about the time she'd begun to drift off again.

She thought she was going to have to beat him off with the pillow.

"I swear to god I'm going to brain you with something, Caleb! I don't want to fuck all night. That was really satisfying—and enough."

He desisted and she composed herself for sleep again. Just about the time she dozed off, he tried another sneak attack.

She shouldn't have given him the idea that that was going to work every time, she thought irritably.

Picking up the pillow beside her, she beat him with it on the head and shoulders until he retreated. He stood beside the bed for some moments while she struggled to go back to sleep and finally climbed in beside her again.

"I'm going to find something harder to beat you on the head with if you wake me up again," she growled. "Sleep or go!"

He seemed a little miffed about it, but he settled down and went to sleep.

Unfortunately, he'd gotten her so riled up it took her a lot longer to drop off again.

All in all, though, she wasn't displeased with her night with Caleb. The sex had been fabulous and the rest—well, she considered that training. She was willing to make an exception now and then and go a couple of rounds, but she was completely satisfied with one. She didn't need two or three—let alone half or all the night—and they were going to have to get that through their thick skulls if they were going to hang around her!

She was really looking forward to intimacy with Korbin!

He was pretty barbaric—his programming and personality were *so* different from either Raathe or Caleb!-- but she thought that might give her an extra thrill.

She had to wait longer to find out, though, than she'd expected. She'd actually begun to think he was going to keep his distance and she might never experience his lovemaking and then one morning out of the blue, when she was bathing, she looked up at a slight sound and found him watching her.

She was so stunned she didn't know what to think—

couldn't think—but he was stark naked and absolutely breathtaking.

* * * *

Korbin's entire plan collapsed when he got to the master cabin and discovered that Tabitha was not in the bed, not asleep. The plan had hinged upon that specific situation—that she would be in bed and asleep.

He could then slip into bed beside her and—while she was still groggy and submissive—he could stroke her breasts until she was aroused.

That was what Caleb had told him anyway when he had suggested that slipping in while she was asleep would make it less likely that she would send him away again. And Raathe had agreed that fondling and kissing her breasts was something she liked very much.

And then from there he need only align his body with hers and ….

Frustration filled him as he stood indecisively by the door.

She was not in bed and not asleep so that plan was useless.

He heard the shower come on as he stood where he was trying to decide whether to simply go away again and wait for a time when he might implement the plan he had made or to see what her reaction might be to finding him in her bed.

He had a bad feeling about that, but the sound of running water jogged a memory.

He had watched Raathe with her in the shower and although he could not see very well because of the water and the angle of the camera and the fog on the glass, he was fairly certain he could replicate that scenario.

Deciding it was worth a try, he crossed the room, but he halted again when he got to the door.

He was fully clothed.

That might make it easier for her to dismiss him, he

decided. Then, too, there was the time lag between asking
and undressing and then executing the scenario.

It might not seem spontaneous if he was forced to do
that and both Raathe and Caleb had said that spontaneity
worked best—or at least the appearance of it. He must do
whatever he was inspired to do and if she did not seem
delighted, he should stop that at once and try something
else. If she appeared thrilled by it, then he should do it
more.

Those instructions seemed simple enough.

She had seemed very happy about Raathe jogging her up
and down his cock. He thought she would be pleased if he
did that. He could certainly not think of any reason why
that would not satisfy when it had before and he was
confident that he would be pleased by it.

He thought as long as he got his cock inside her he
would be happy.

Resentment flickered through him as he stripped.

If that smirking bastard, Caleb, was not such a dick and
had shared his programming he would feel more confident
because then he would be certain that he knew what to do
to please his woman. Now he could only guess and rely
upon visual lessons he had managed to gather.

Shaking that thought, he opened the door before he had
time to rethink the matter, and stepped inside.

Obviously, she heard his entrance. She flicked a glance
toward the door and did a double take and then her eyes
widened like saucers.

Korbin felt his cock wilt at that expression and looked
down in dismay. What the fuck? The gods damn bastard
had hardly lain down since they had started the voyage and
he had thought there might be a chance to fuck Tabitha and
now it decided to fucking lay down when there was an
actual possibility?

What the hell was he to do with it if it would not stand
again?

Tabitha was still looking at him when he looked up again, but the frozen look had vanished. He was not entirely certain of what the look that replaced it might mean.

It did not look welcoming to his mind.

But, to his relief, as he moved toward the shower, she made room for him, moving to one end.

He hoped that was what she was doing and not retreating with nowhere to go.

He stepped inside and discovered it was almost as if he had stepped through some sort of portal or time warp. His mind went perfectly blank. Struggle though he might to recall the scenario he had determined he could and would replicate, he could not.

He could only stare at Tabitha in stunned admiration, feeling his body heat up so fast it seemed to fry his brain. He was standing perfectly still and yet his heart and lungs began to strain as if he was running full out until he began to feel some concern that he might merely pass out from overloading his system.

Particularly when she lifted her hand and began to scrub his chest.

She said something, but it was muffled in his ears as if he was hearing her from under water—because his heartbeat was so loud there he could hear very little else.

And then she slipped.

And Korbin grabbed her waist to support her and steady her.

Chapter Fourteen

Instantly, memories flooded Korbin's mind, the memories he had been so frantically searching for.

He lifted Tabitha straight up, pressed her against the wall behind her, and covered her mouth in ravenous seduction that skated the fine edge of violence, exploring the exquisitely tender inner surfaces of her mouth possessively.

Tabitha curled her arms around his shoulders and her legs around his waist, accepting conquest, so thrilled with it she was almost as mindless as he was. He had crashed upon her senses so explosively that she was almost instantly inundated, lost in a molten sea of desire. She was drunk on the taste and feel of him, reeling with his scent and touch and still unable to fill her needs fast enough.

She clutched at him, pressed more tightly to him, desperate for as much contact skin to skin as she could manage.

She'd grown so accustomed to him she'd ceased to be impressed by the massiveness of him—until that moment in time when she was engulfed by him—thrilled to mindlessness by him.

With no thought processes involved, she reached blindly for his cock by instinct alone. Intent on mounting it, she'd just managed to brush it with her fingers when he broke from her lips and lifted her higher to knead her breasts and pull on her nipples with hard drags of his mouth that made her kegels clap in demand and the walls of her sex weep for his possession.

He kissed and fondled her breasts until she thought she was going to lose her mind—or pass out from all the panting for breath.

She was on fire.

And she could only think of one way to put it out.

Thankfully, that finally occurred to Korbin. He ceased

to torment her breasts then and commenced to trying to stuff his mammoth into her hole. The sting of stretching skin brought her, briefly, to the edge of sanity again, but she was too far gone to be deterred from their goal by a little pain.

She tried to find leverage to help him breach the mouth and couldn't.

Luckily, though, her efforts put Korbin in mind of the need for leverage and he broke off abruptly and stepped out of the shower with her.

The blast of cold when the air touched her wet skin restored enough brain function for her to figure out he was headed to the bed with her mounted on the head of his cock like a hood ornament. She gripped him tighter to prevent herself from sliding off when he bent over and half crawled onto the bed with her.

The brief disconnect from the move disappointed her, but he began battering at her almost immediately and not only managed to reconnect, but thoroughly embedded the head of his cock several inches deep.

Unfortunately, the head of his cock was gloriously smaller than the shaft. Plugging in still left a major portion of the fight to claim the battlefield in the wind.

Thankfully, he had no 'give up' in him or a lot of patience for the battle to claim. He strained and retreated only a handful of times before he managed to triumph and drive so deeply Tabitha thought he might have punctured her womb for a millisecond.

Which made it borderline bizarre that the pain seemed to set off her climax.

Or maybe it just wasn't sufficient to block it?

Whatever the case, she jetted right off into space almost the instant he managed to completely claim her channel and the clutching motion of her muscles ripped his control from him so that he came on the heels of her ride to rapture.

She tightened her grip on him as the shudders wracked

him so hard he grunted as if in pain.

And then he went completely limp as if he'd passed out.

Tabitha gloried in it for all of two seconds.

But then she began to feel as if he was going to crush her into the floor beneath the mattress.

"Korbin?"

He grunted—clearly still unable to formulate comprehensible speech.

"I can't breathe."

He literally leapt off of her the instant she gasped those three little words into his ear.

She sucked in a deep, relieved breath when he did and smiled dreamily. "Let's cuddle just a minute."

She saw he was looking confused when she managed to pry her eyelid up.

She almost dismissed it, but it occurred to her that he would have no way of knowing or understanding such a request and wouldn't learn unless she was willing to teach him.

She got him to align himself on the bed more properly. Then she arranged him to suit herself, curled next to him and pulled his arms around her. Grasping the damp covers, she pulled them over both of them.

"The covers are wet," he pointed out in a voice still deep and husky.

It sent a shiver through her. "That happens when you don't dry off first."

"How long should I cuddle you?"

Irritation flickered through her. "Until I'm ready to get up."

"You will tell me?"

Tabitha counted to ten. "Yes, baby."

He was silent for several moments. "I am not a baby. I am a soldier."

"But you're my baby."

He digested that in silence for several minutes. "Does

that mean I did not pleasure you?"

She gave him an affectionate squeeze. "It means you did—very much."

The tension went out of him. She hadn't even realized that he was lying tensely beside her until that moment when he relaxed.

A few minutes later, just as she was really getting in to the intimate moments, she heard him snore.

Torn between amusement and irritation, she debated giving up on the idea of impressing upon him what cuddling meant and how to do it properly, and finally shrugged it off and settled to doze herself.

He reached for her breast just as she was skating the edge of peace.

She popped his fingers, shoved his arms off, bounded out of bed and stalked to the bathroom to finish her shower.

It was a momentary displeasure, though. Overall, she had been thrilled with her time with Korbin and beyond that she thought it might bring some peace to their little group if no one was sexually frustrated on top of being bored to death.

There were still fights in the hold, unfortunately, but they seemed to be far less violent and far less frequent as long as she kept them 'tamed' by accepting them in her bed every week or so—on rotation.

She was happy to do it—as long as it didn't present a hardship for her, and it didn't as long as they took no for an answer when she wasn't in the mood.

They bumped along fairly well until they were nearing their destination. Then, for some reason unknown to Tabitha, they had the mother of all battles in the hold and damned near destroyed the ship.

* * * *

Raathe didn't explode immediately, but that was because he was too stunned, at first, to take it all in. "You did what?"

Korbin tensed at the tone, studying Raathe intently for signs of an imminent explosion before he repeated his report. "I sent out a message to any of our comrades who might be on Destiny and could arrange passage to the Nation for us."

Raathe glanced at Caleb to see if he had heard the same.

Caleb shrugged, but there was a look of consternation in his expression that suggested he had heard what Raathe thought he had.

"Without asking? Without discussion? You have taken it upon yourself to risk everyone on board by sending a message so that we might have a welcoming committee waiting to blow us away when we get there?"

Korbin felt his face heat with discomfort. "We have discussed this many times since I brought it up! I thought we were in agreement."

"I did not agree to a fucking thing!" Raathe bellowed. "I said that I would consider it!"

"I did not agree either!" Caleb put in.

Korbin punched him. "Stay out of it!"

"I am part of this family! I have a right to speak!"

"He has a right to voice his opinion!" Raathe growled, punching Korbin for punching Caleb.

"We should take this to the hold," Caleb said decisively. Getting up and moving to the door of the hold, he opened it.

Korbin, who'd followed, kicked him in the ass as soon as he bent over to start down the ladder.

Caleb missed the ladder and landed face down on the floor of the hold.

He leapt down behind him before Raathe had the chance to 'assist' him in his descent.

Raathe landed on top of him, bearing him to the floor and then punching him in the face repeatedly until Korbin managed to buck him off.

He scrambled to his feet before Raathe could recover

and put some distance between them. "I did not use the regular channel that the humans use," he snarled. "Nor a frequency that they are able to hear even if they should stumble upon that channel. And beyond that, I sent the message in code."

Caleb kicked him in the back of his knee, forcing the leg to give out. Before Korbin could catch his balance, Raathe leapt on him again, grabbed him by one arm and slung him across the room so that he slammed into the wall/bulkhead.

They had been pounding upon one another for almost thirty minutes and slinging one another into the walls when Caleb diverted them.

"Uh oh. I think you broke something," he said in a voice filled with enough dread that it instantly pierced Raathe and Korbin's preoccupation with mutual destruction.

Staggering with fatigue, the two broke off their battle and moved to see what it was that they had destroyed.

They discovered that there were strange, flat squares lying all over the floor.

"What is it?" Raathe asked uneasily.

Caleb shrugged. "I do not know. I have not seen the like before. But it fell out of this crack in the panel after you drove Korbin's head into it. Do you think it might be critical to the ship's integrity?"

Frowning since Raathe actually had no data regarding the ship beyond what he had gleaned from the flight manual, he moved his hand to the fracture he had made cautiously. He could not feel that air was escaping, however. Bending down, he peered inside and discovered that there were a number of the things stuffed into the crevice haphazardly enough he decided it was something that had been hidden rather than any part of the structure.

Somewhat relieved, he crouched to study the rectangles more closely. They were smooth and made of a material he was unfamiliar with.

Printed very clearly on one, however, was the name Cpl. John Raathe.

Shock slammed into him hard enough to rock him off his feet. He fell back against the bulkhead, pounded with images that went through his mind like a whirlwind.

Caleb had spotted the name, too. He picked the object up. When he did, he discovered it was a pocket of some kind. Dozens of light, hair-thin squares fell out and drifted to the floor. Words in black lettering covered them. He picked one up and studied it.

"This is strange material. It is almost as light as air and yet it holds these words like a computer display. It does not react to my touch."

Raathe clutched his head until the pain subsided. When it did, he reached for the sheets on the floor and gathered them up. "It is paper," he said, grasping the deeply buried information and dragging it to light.

"Some new technology?" Caleb asked curiously.

"No. Very old. Decades."

"Each of these pocket things have papers in them," Korbin said. "And each has a name on the outside."

Raathe hardly heard him. He was staring at the file that had his name on it—Cpl. John Raathe—trying to sort through the memories finding them had unearthed. When he realized that efforts to capture them was useless, he arranged the papers by number and began to read them.

Caleb and Korbin both selected files and settled to read.

"I was born," Raathe said after a few moments when he had read them all. "I was given the name John Raathe in the orphanage where I grew up. And I became a corporal when I was a soldier.

"Before I died on the battlefield."

Korbin tilted his head, studying him curiously. "These died also. They were frozen for return for their funerals, but they were shipped to Robotics Inc., instead."

"These also," Caleb said, frowning. "It seems strange

that these were all born humans and they were also all orphans."

"It is not strange at all," Raathe said angrily. "They were chosen because they had no one to complain when their bodies were not returned."

"Well! It is very strange that they were shipped to Robotics Inc, isn't it?"

"That would depend on why they were shipped there," Raathe responded, searching the files on the floor and then getting up and ripping the paneling loose so that all of the others spilled out.

Lastly, a data stick fell from the cubby.

Raathe picked it up and headed upstairs to the flight console.

Korbin and then a short time later, Caleb, followed him.

It really didn't take very long at all to piece together the story once they had read all of the files. The data stick contained duplicates of the physical files they'd found plus thousands more digital files, all of them the background information of the men who'd been sent to Robotics Inc. and came out as cyborgs—product of the company that had landed the biggest government contract in history.

As appalling as that was there were hints that not all of the soldiers they'd received were actually dead before they were put in cryo.

So—not just the unethical disposal of human remains, not just a complete disregard for men who had made the ultimate sacrifice for that their country—slavery and murder.

For money.

As far as they could tell, Langston had no knowledge of how it was that the company managed to develop and produce cyborgs light years ahead of their competition.

Not at first.

But he had discovered the secret and agreed to hush money. So he was guilty after the fact, but he also had plausible deniability. And he had evidence on everyone else.

This was what they'd tried to kill him for, Raathe realized.

They'd realized it was only a matter of time before their secret was out—unless they could get their hands on the proof and destroy it—especially when their attempt to make up for the losses by gearing up production of factory bots backfired.

They hadn't thought the factory workers would *dare* to challenge their decisions. They were too poor to have a voice and too fearful of losing the little they had.

The people at the top had failed to consider what would happen if they took the little the poor had and left them with nothing at all—total revolt!

"Do you think Tabitha had any idea what was going on?" Caleb asked unhappily.

Raathe stared at him, casting his mind back over the years. It was with relief that he shook his head. "It would not matter to me if she knew. She would not have been born when this happened. She was a small child when I was sold to Langston. She could not even have had a hand in hiding the information. And it would not matter to me even if she did know. I would still love her as much as ever."

Caleb was clearly relieved.

Korbin looked so relieved that he almost looked a little sick to his stomach.

Raathe was so numb for a time he was not certain how he felt about any of it—beyond anger and disgust that humans could do such a thing only for the sake of money. As the numbness wore off, though, he realized that what he felt most was gratitude. If they had not done what they had, he would have long since returned to dust and he would not have had the chance to awaken to a world with Tabitha in it. He was profoundly grateful for that.

In truth, he had left nothing and no one behind in exchange for something far beyond anything he had had hope of before.

Korbin pierced his self-absorption.

"I would be afraid for her if she was involved. That would not change the way I feel about her either, but it could put her in danger with others. We should destroy it."

Raathe considered that and shook his head. "This proves she had nothing to do with it. We cannot destroy it or allow it to be destroyed. If it came out anyway, then we would not have a way to prove her innocent."

Korbin paled. "I had not thought of that."

"I am so certain that it is vital to keep it that I believe we must make copies and each carry one to insure we do not find ourselves without if it becomes necessary for her protection."

They went back into the hold after that and returned the physical files to their hiding place and carefully concealed them once more.

Korbin hated to bring it up when they had already fought over it, but the matter needed to be settled and very soon because they were getting very close to Destiny. "What have you decided regarding that other matter?"

Raathe frowned. "The file stated that all of the first cyborgs created were fitted with a self-destruct feature. I feel confident this is what has been causing the sharp pains in my brain, but it is no comfort to know that I was right and that it could kill me. Possibly the nanos are all that have prevented it from being activated. Would someone there, on the cyborg world, be able to remove it?"

Korbin thought that over. "We have a number of trained physicians—human and cyborg—and we have put together the best medical centers we can. I could not guarantee it, but I believe it is possible."

Raathe nodded. "Then that would be the safest place for us to go, I think—best for Tabitha, best for us. We will just have to convince her of that. Mayhap when she has read all of this it will help to convince her."

Korbin frowned. "She has agreed to be our mate. Surely she expects to go there with us since we told her that was the plan?"

Raathe shook his head. "When you know her as well as I then you will not assume that she will do something only because she has said that she will."

Chapter Fifteen

Tabitha had mixed feelings as the compound came into view. In a sense she was relieved as she always was when she finished a journey. It would be good to get back on solid ground even if it was different ground.

But she would be parting company with the guys here and she hadn't realized until this moment how much she cared about them.

Of course, it was the fact that she did care that she had decided that she just couldn't go with them. She'd always liked to think of herself as being in fantastic shape, but at peak condition no human could compare to a cyborg.

She would be a stone around their neck and they would

have to keep their wits about them to survive. They were very likely going to be hunted forever more.

And if that wasn't bad enough, she had come to realize that she was pregnant—as wonderful, unbelievable, scary as that was—and that meant slowing them down even more, becoming more of a danger to them as time went on.

She had to think of the baby's best interests, too. She couldn't risk his life just so she could be with the guys a little longer.

And she felt that she would be if she tried to go with them.

He would be her compensation for having to give up his father—Raathe. She knew it was Raathe's baby. She felt it in her heart.

She was fiercely glad of that.

And at the same time sad that she would never have Caleb's child or Korbin's. But she thought they would find a woman who would give them what they wanted and deserved.

It didn't actually matter whether it was true or not that they'd attained awareness. What mattered was that they believed and they wanted the life of a sentient being— complete with family.

She didn't know if they'd be able to do that or not. Raathe had started life as a human and been made into a machine and that was the main reason she was convinced the child was his.

That plus his absolute determination and dedication to producing one on her.

Caleb and Korbin probably had as much human genetic materials as Raathe or almost as much, but they hadn't begun life as a human being. They'd been created in a lab and she wasn't convinced they could reproduce or ever would be able to—not naturally, anyway. They could certainly contribute some of their DNA to making a child, but … in the lab as they'd been created, not in the womb of a woman.

She didn't expect them to take it well.

They were stubborn as hell.

That was why she hadn't mentioned it to them, had no intention of telling them her plans weren't the same as theirs.

She thought any kind of debate would be useless. They wouldn't accept. They would argue and then they would take control. She was going to have to betray their trust to do what she thought was the 'right thing', the best, for all concerned.

She hadn't figured out exactly how she was going to manage that, but that was because she thought she would have to see exactly what kind of situation she was going to have to deal with before she could make any decisions.

She thought she might contact her father's lawyers and see what they might be able to do to get her out of the mess she'd gotten herself in to. She thought if she could just get probation, she could live with that.

She wasn't having her baby in prison, though.

And she wasn't handing him over to someone else while she spent time in prison.

That was completely unacceptable.

A deal would make it possible to resume the life she'd had—at least to a degree.

No deal meant she was going to have to make a life on Destiny with the rest of the escaped criminals and that didn't have a huge appeal. She might not have a choice, but she wanted to explore any options before she settled.

Her focus was interrupted by a flicker of movement in the courtyard enclosed by the security walls surrounding her father's estate. Almost on top of that, alarms began to sound on the ship.

It flashed through her mind that someone had launched a missile at them from her father's compound!

Korbin charged out of the cockpit, snatched her up, and

raced to the tail end of the ship. He had barely dropped her into the secure seat there and grabbed the security harness when something slammed into the ship hard enough to pitch him right over her head and into the wall above her.

She slammed into him and ricocheted back into the seat. He hit the floor in front of her and then the far wall.

Tabitha managed to grab the harness and halfway secure herself into the seat.

Korbin dragged himself back across the room. Dropping to his knees, he curled his arms around her and locked his fingers at the back of the seat.

Tabitha had no clue of what his intention was, but he was crushing her!

It didn't occur to her to complain, though.

And then she realized as something crashed into him and he grunted as the air was forced from his chest that he was trying to shield her with his body from the flying objects of the disintegrating ship at impact.

She felt like she was in a blender even with Korbin's protection. She didn't know if it would have been better if he hadn't tried to protect her or worse.

Finally, the ship stopped moving, however—thankfully!

In the aftermath, Tabitha was too stunned to feel any pain if there was damage. Shock had snatched her senses away from her. She could barely hear or see or feel. It was as if she was wrapped in cotton.

Korbin fell off of her.

Consternation filled her but even that was distant, muffled.

Then she discovered that Raathe was standing over her. He dropped to his knees to examine her and then ripped the safety harness off and carefully gathered her to his chest.

Korbin managed to stagger to his feet as Raathe turned and began trying to wade through the debris surrounding them. They met Caleb on the other side of what had been the doorway to the master cabin. Like Korbin and Raathe, he was bleeding from cuts on his head and arms—and probably elsewhere.

Raathe shoved her against Caleb's chest. He grabbed her instinctively. "Carry her. I will need my hands free to fight."

Fight, Tabitha thought blankly. Who? Why?

Almost as if he had read her mind, he pointed out that their ship had been shot down by a missile—launched from inside her father's compound. Korbin managed to make it to the weapons locker and emptied it, dividing the contents between himself and Raathe.

"Stay back," Raathe ordered Caleb as he and Korbin stepped cautiously to the opening ripped in one side of the ship. Almost the second they appeared, bullets began to pelt the interior.

Caleb whirled around with her and whipped a look in both directions, searching for safety that wasn't there. Finally, he moved toward the cockpit with her as Raathe and Korbin made a new hole and returned fire.

There was a human-like scream and a loud grunt from outside and then more bullets flew into the ship.

Raathe ripped the back off of a seat and used it as a shield as he stepped through the opening to have a clearer shot.

The battle raged for maybe ten minutes and then Korbin returned. "Bring her. Raathe has breached the wall."

Raathe hadn't actually 'breached'. He'd leapt to the top. He was crouched there, scanning the courtyard when Caleb carried her from the wreckage. As she glanced at him, he dropped from sight on the other side.

Korbin took her from Caleb as they reached the wall. If she'd had any idea what he had in mind, she might have protested but there was no time for her to think through what was about to happen let alone protest. Korbin bent his knees and crouched low and then used that force to propel them to the top of the wall. They barely paused before he dropped down beside Raathe. Caleb landed a split second after they did.

And a split second after that, a hail of bullets peppered their position.

Instantly, the guys formed a protective shell around her, moving to stand shoulder to shoulder.

Tabitha was so completely cut off that she couldn't see anything.

She could hear very well, though. The projectiles raining down on them didn't slack off for many minutes that seemed like hours. When it did, she knew that that was because some of the people firing had stopped to reload.

Raathe tried to use the lull to find cover, but they didn't manage to reach it before the shooting resumed in fierceness.

"Fall down, you stupid bastards!" someone bellowed.

Almost as if at that command, Korbin fell. Taking her with him, he managed to drag her halfway beneath him and covered her with his free arm and leg.

And then he went perfectly still.

Tabitha's heart seemed to stop when he did. "Korbin?" She gripped his uniform, tried to find a pulse. "Oh my god, Korbin!"

Caleb fell almost on top of them, crashing headlong beside her. She screamed his name, but there was no response, no movement when his body finally sank fully to the ground.

Raathe dropped to his knees and fell back.

Tabitha was too stunned by that time even to react. She had no idea when the shooting stopped. She was too focused on trying to climb out from under the men to see how badly they were hurt.

Abruptly, Raathe sat up and fell sideways.

At least that was what her brain interpreted the movement to be until she discovered they were surrounded by armed men and that it was the men dragging Raathe,

Caleb, and Korbin away from her.

She fought them then, struggling to reach Raathe. She managed to get to him and pull his head onto her lap. He was unresponsive and tears welled in her eyes. Her throat closed as if a giant hand was trying to squeeze the life out of her. "Raathe?" she managed to say in a croaking whisper. "Baby? Don't be dead! Please?"

"He can't be dead. He wasn't alive to start with. Get her away from them and get rid of them."

Tabitha whirled toward the voice. She was blinded by her tears, but she knew that voice. "Father?" she gasped, blinking the tears from her eyes.

"Are you alright?" he asked.

Fury washed over her in a wave. "You *bastard*! *You* shot us down?"

"Believe me, I had no idea that you were on board. All I knew was that my ship was stolen and the thieves were about to land in my backyard."

"You lying son-of-a-bitch!" Tabitha screamed, launching herself at him with every intention of shredding him with her nails. "You killed them, you bastard!"

Her father thwarted her by catching her wrists before she could do more than rake her nails over his face once. "You're hysterical. Medic! Give her something! They can't be dead when they were never alive, Tabitha! They're cyborgs. But you always had trouble seeing that, didn't you?"

Tabitha barely felt the prick as she was injected, but the sedative very quickly took the fight out of her and dragged her into a black pit.

Langston watched as she crumpled to the ground and then nodded at the medic. "Put her in her room. But lock the doors and make sure the window shutters are secure. You can be certain she'll try to get out when she comes to."

He turned to watch the men trying to drag off the cyborgs they'd taken down. "Leave that for now and go

search the wreckage for those files. I need them. Make
damn sure you don't come back without them."

He watched until they'd left the compound and then
turned and went back inside.

The scratches on his face burned like hell. He headed to
the med center to look for something to soothe and to
disinfect. No telling what she might have picked up and
infections on this rock were serious and quite often fatal.

Stupid little cunt! He should have known she would cut
up ugly about him disposing of her sex toys!

She'd gone off the deep end, he supposed, after her
mother died. Never had been right since. The psychiatrists
he'd had treat her had assured him that she was just
struggling to cope and she would eventually 'outgrow' her
fantasy about their security cyborg being real.

He'd never had much faith in the bastards! Waste of
money. But he had been sentimental enough at the time to
think it was worth a try to get the treatment.

Easy to see what had come of that.

By the time he'd managed to thoroughly clean the
scratches and anoint them with salve, he'd managed to put
the look of hatred in her eyes from his mind. She'd always
looked at him that way any time she was thwarted, he told
himself.

Never before with quite that degree, but then she was no
fool. She knew he'd at least suspected she was onboard
when he'd had the ship shot down. He supposed instead of
pretending he hadn't known it might have been better to
explain that he'd had that shot very carefully calculated for
the minimum of damage it would take to bring it down—to
make certain she had the best chance of surviving it. That
he couldn't take the chance that they would realize he was
laying in wait for them and take off again with his
insurance! He needed those damned files! And he'd
known when they circled the place that they were
suspicious of a trap.

He shook his head in disgust. Didn't it just figure? He'd hung on to the fucking things for years because he'd known he would need them, eventually, given the people he was dealing with. And now that he needed them ….

He supposed he should have kept Raathe instead of disposing of him, but he'd begun to behave erratically enough he thought keeping Raathe might be more′ dangerous than getting rid of him.

Well, he was gone now. Good riddance to bad rubbish!

* * * *

Ranger Dallas moved the crawler close to the bodies, parked it, and got out. Nodding to his partner, Ranger Reese, he grasped the feet of the first while his partner grasped the shoulders and they moved the first into the hold. They moved Korbin last.

It took them longer than he'd expected—heavy bastards—but they still managed it before anyone thought to question the removal and piled into the crawler and pulled out.

The rest of Langston's posse was still busy combing through the wreckage when they left.

They were halfway back to town before there was any sort of sound from the back. "Korbin? That you?" Ranger Dallas called back.

Korbin grunted. It was all he could manage.

"Did either of the others make it?"

Korbin struggled for a few moments to lift one arm so that he could check, but he finally gave up and sought the nothingness that had enveloped him before.

Reese exchanged a hard look with Dallas. "Might have been a case of too little, too late."

Dallas shook his head. "I don't know about the other two, but Korbin made it through Xeno-12. He can make it through this. It might take a while for the nanos to repair all the damage, but I'm almost certain they will."

Reese nodded. "Maybe."

They discovered when they got to the safe house that the three were still completely unresponsive. Releasing a gusty sigh, they dragged the three out and carried them inside. When they'd settled them, they set up drip feeds to supply them with the energy they would need to recover—if they were going to, and then left them, carefully locking up the safe house behind them.

"You were on Xeno-12?" Reese asked when they left.

"Nope. You know I'm a hunter. I met Korbin when they sent me to kill him."

"Good thing for them that you recognized him."

Dallas shrugged. "I knew he would be there. He contacted me—sort of—to ask for passage to the Nation."

Reese sent him a startled look. "And you still took part?"

"What the fuck else could I do? Blow our cover? We're no damned good to anybody if they find out what we're doing here."

Reese shrugged. "You might have let me in on it."

"I would have if I had realized right away that it was them. Langston caught me off guard shooting them down."

"That bastard is insane! You think he knew his daughter was onboard?"

"I think I wouldn't have taken the chance if it was my daughter," Dallas said tightly.

Chapter Sixteen

Tabitha roused enough to realize she was on an examination table being scanned. Consternation filled her. Her father would know about the baby ....

But she discovered she simply didn't have anything to fight with and sank into oblivion once more.

When she woke again, she was lying in her bed—in a room that looked identical to the one she'd had in her father's mansion on Earth. It was so identical, she was briefly utterly baffled, felt as if her mind might have snapped.

How could she be at home?

Was it even possible that she could have such an elaborate hallucination?

A server bot roused her when it entered the room through a small, nearly invisible door, in the wainscoting carrying a tray of food.

"Dinner is served, Mistress Tabitha," the bot said in a halting, metallic voice.

Dinner? Of what day, she wondered? How long had she been out?

She damned sure hadn't been asleep. She'd been drugged.

That thought brought her mind to the baby and horror washed over her in a cold wave. She cupped her belly. It was still slightly rounded, but she hadn't been far enough along to feel the baby move. She didn't know if it was alright or not.

The urge to burst into tears swept through her, nearly overwhelmed her.

But she couldn't bear thinking about her losses. She just couldn't deal with it at the moment. She pushed it deep into the darkness of her mind and held it there.

She had to think about herself now—because if she didn't make it her baby wouldn't.

He might not anyway. They might already have killed him, but she had to act on the possibility that he was alright and that there was something she could do to protect him.

That thought brought her to the food the bot had deposited.

She hadn't eaten in so long her belly felt painfully empty. She had to eat, had to keep body and soul together even though she felt as if her soul had already fled with Raathe—with Caleb and Korbin.

She *had* accepted them as her mates, she realized, or she wouldn't feel so crushed with grief she could hardly think. She'd just lied to herself that she was only considering it, that she was pretending to appease them.

She'd lied to herself about considering options. She'd bonded with them.

She sucked in a deep breath and held it, fighting to keep herself together.

When she thought she'd mastered the urge to fall apart, she sat up and moved the tray to her lap.

The food under the covered dishes looked almost too beautiful to eat—and even so a wave of nausea washed over her. Ignoring her belly's rebelliousness, she picked up the croissant and buttered it and then took a small bite. Her salivary glands cramped painfully as the taste filled her mouth. She grimaced, paused for the pain to pass and then chewed and swallowed.

She'd managed to eat maybe half when her father came into the room.

"You're doing better, I see," he said coolly.

Tabitha pretended he wasn't there and he hadn't spoken. Otherwise, she wasn't certain she could have stopped herself from attacking him with her fork and trying to dig his black heart out of his chest.

He crossed the room to stand beside the bed. "Where are the files?"

Tabitha lifted her head and studied him for a long

moment, trying to decide whether to tell him or not. "Raathe had them," she said finally.

He actually turned white, but she wasn't fooled into thinking it was any kind of remorse for what he'd done and she couldn't resist stabbing at him. "Uh oh. Guess that means you had him burned. Too bad."

He slapped her so hard it made her ears ring.

It hurt like hell, too, but she was so shocked that he'd actually struck her she didn't even feel it at first.

As many times as they'd locked horns, he had *never* struck her before.

That tore it for her, severed the last fragile thread to him as far as she was concerned.

"You ungrateful bitch! After all I've done for you! I *needed* those god damned files!"

"You killed them—Raathe, Caleb—Korbin! You fucking bastard! I hope they torture you to death for those fucking files when they catch up to you!"

He lifted his hand to strike again, but Tabitha was ready that time. She snatched her fork up and held it like a knife, prepared to strike if he did.

He studied it for a long moment and then lowered his hand. Turning on his heels abruptly, he strode from the room.

A sob escaped her, but she sucked it up, refusing to cry about his mistreatment when she hadn't even allowed herself to grieve over the guys.

She heard the lock click when he closed the door.

Not that she had doubted for a moment that she was a prisoner.

It was his *modus operandi*. Any time he was displeased with her for something he considered that she'd done to thwart him, he locked her away to think about what was going to happen next.

And 'next' was inevitably more unpleasant.

Well, she didn't plan on hanging around.

She was grown now.

She'd learned a *lot* about breaking into and out of places!

Releasing a pent up breath, she dropped the fork and rounded up the food that had been scattered across the bed when her father had slapped her. She needed it, needed her strength. Escaping wasn't going to be easy.

* * * *

Korbin and Caleb were up and pacing the floor before awareness finally seeped into Raathe's mind and he found himself floating up toward consciousness. His last memory—the battle—was instantly on his mind as he rose toward the surface, though, and he came around swinging.

Korbin dodged him with little effort, but he managed to lay Caleb out with a glancing blow to the jaw.

"You are awake. Good! I had begun think we would have to leave you," Korbin said coolly.

Feeling as if he was coming down from a three day drunken brawl, Raathe said nothing as he cradled his head in his hands and tried to recall what he could that had happened before ....

"Tabby!" he exclaimed abruptly, surging halfway up from the bench where he had been laying and whipping a look around the small area.

"Her father has her," Caleb said flatly, working his jaw as he sat up and then picked himself up off the floor.

"He has his posse out searching for us. Or more specifically, the data stick that you have. The Hunters that saved our asses are gone to arrange passage. We have a small window to collect Tabitha and then we must go."

"I will not leave her with that bastard!" Raathe growled, heading for the only door. "You two go if you cannot wait."

Korbin fell into step behind him. "She is my woman, too. Besides, you were unconscious. I know the way."

"I have her tracker code. I will find her."

Caleb didn't bother trying to convince either of the others. He passed them and climbed into the crawler that had been left for them.

They joined him a few minutes later, started the crawler, and headed out.

It was dusk when they left the shelter where they had lain until their nanos could repair the damage to them from the shoot out. Raathe had taken point and sustained far more damage because of that, which had required a longer recovery. "How long has she been there?" he asked as they headed across the desert toward her father's compound.

"Five day cycles according to Dallas when he brought the transport and the information about the arrangements they have made."

"Fuck!" Raathe growled. "You should not have waited for me to go after her."

"We did not wait," Caleb said. "We were only able to reach full function a few hours ago."

"And I did not think my chances of success would be enhanced by taking him," Korbin added.

Caleb glared at him, but then thought it over and shrugged. "I do not have soldier programming. You could have allowed me to access ...."

"I have no sex droid programming and you will not allow me to access that. I see no reason to share if you will not trade."

Raathe stopped the crawler in a deep gulley and got out. Grabbing up scrubby vegetation, he piled it around the camo-painted vehicle. Korbin and Caleb followed more slowly. Korbin gathered vegetation to help.

Caleb stood in one place and scanned the rolling desert around them. "I see nothing. Why have we stopped here?"

"The compound is just beyond that rise there."

Caleb squinted at it in the gathering gloom. "That is miles away," he said pointedly. "Why stop here? This will take a good bit longer. And Dallas said they would not be able to wait after the meeting time."

Korbin popped him on the back of the head. The sound ricocheted around them like a thunderclap. "Sound carries a very long way stupid! They would hear the crawler if we tried to get closer."

"They will hear you two stupid asses if you keep that up," Raathe growled, striding away.

"When we get to the cyborg world, I will find the programming for the soldier cyborgs and then I will kick your stupid ass," Caleb growled.

Korbin snorted. "You may think that."

They fell silent as they crossed the terrain that separated them from Tabitha, focused after that challenge on getting to her and freeing her as quickly as possible.

Apparently, it was true that the men employed as guards were out searching for Raathe, because the compound was virtually empty beyond a couple of sentries on the wall. Raathe and Korbin left Caleb and crept up to the wall, positioned themselves beneath the guard stations and took both out soundlessly. Leaving the two propped up to appear to still be functioning guards, they met across from the shuttered, second floor bedroom. "She will be in there," Raathe said quietly and confidently.

Korbin frowned. "You are certain it is not a trap?"

Raathe smiled grimly. "I can hear her working on the lock."

Korbin tilted his head, listening. "I had wondered what that was."

"And it is the only room that has shutters closed and locked. Unless he has bound and gagged her, this will be her."

Korbin nodded and crouched to study the wall of the building. "The ledge is barely enough for a finger hold.

"That will be enough," Raathe responded grimly. He studied the distance and calculated the velocity he would have to use to leap the distance between the outside wall to

the building and then leapt. Catching the window ledge
with his fingers, he allowed himself to hang from them for
a moment and then reached up to catch the edge of the
shutter.

It came away with an ungodly scream of wrenched
metal. Tabitha was standing on the other side, a fork in her
hand, her eyes wide and bulging with horror. Raathe
pushed her aside and climbed in.

"Raathe?" she gasped. "Oh my god! I thought you
were dead."

"Close. We will talk when we are away. Are you
ready?"

Tabitha sniffed her tears back and nodded, too stunned
to even consider offering an argument.

Raathe hesitated and then pulled the data stick from his
pocket and held it up questioningly. It took Tabitha a few
minutes to figure out what he was asking. "Whatever you
want to do is fine with me. I love you."

Raathe strode to the bedside table and placed the data
stick on the surface. When he returned, he hoisted Tabitha
to the ledge and climbed up beside her. Recalculating the
weight and velocity, he leapt with her that time. Korbin
was waiting to steady them on the top of the wall when
they landed and then the three of them leapt from the wall
to the ground.

Caleb joined them as they took off at a run in the
direction they'd come from.

They had only covered perhaps a dozen yards,
unfortunately, when shots were fired from the compound—
a guard they'd missed or her father. Tabitha had no clue.
She was done with him. She wasn't sorry that Raathe had
left the data stick for him, but she wouldn't have blamed
him if he hadn't—or cared what the consequences might be
for her father.

He made his own decisions without regard to anyone
else. He should pay for his decisions like everyone else

had to.

They managed to get out of range of the gunfire before anyone was hit, but as they gained the distance that allowed them to see the front of the compound, they saw the jounce of lights on a vehicle approaching.

"Fuck!" Raathe growled. Snatching Tabitha off her feet and tossing her over his shoulder, he began to run full out. Korbin and Caleb followed suit although Korbin periodically turned to make sure they were keeping a safe distance from the threat.

"They are gaining," he said after a few minutes.

"Do we have more weapons in the crawler? Anything big enough to slow them or stop them?"

"Negative," Korbin responded. "I will drop back and hold them."

"No!" Tabitha gasped with an effort. "I thought I'd lost y'all. I can't deal with that! Please? Let's just go."

Raathe hesitated.

"We are close to the crawler now," Caleb pointed out. "It will give us more protection."

Raathe calculated the timing. "It will be close," he said grimly.

"Yes. This is what I think, too," Korbin said.

Raathe hesitated. "Korbin, get in and get it started!" he said finally. "Caleb—you will have to take rear guard and shield Tabitha."

Caleb dropped back a couple of yards and took a position directly behind Raathe, or more specifically, Tabitha. Korbin pulled ahead and raced to the crawler. They heard it start up moments before they reached the gulley.

Raathe and Caleb skidded to a grinding halt beside the vehicle, flung the doors open, and leapt in.

Korbin slammed the power pedal to the floor and pulled the crawler in a tight circle that nearly threw them out the door again. Raathe caught Tabitha and plopped her into a seat and then slammed the door.

The tangent of the gulley was almost ninety degrees to the path they'd taken to reach the vehicle—the same path their pursuers had taken. By following it, they closed the distance somewhat, but they were low enough to be out of line of sight and managed to put a good distance between them before the enemy vehicle crashed into the gulley in the dark.

It seemed to be enough of a delay to give them the lead they needed, but they didn't slow until they reached the rendezvous point. Dallas and Reese had the ship prepped for launch when they arrived.

"Thought we were going to be making this trip without passengers," Dallas called back to them with graveyard humor as they raced up the gangplank.

"Grab your seats, jump into your harness, or kiss your ass goodbye," Reese advised from the control room. "We launch in ten seconds! And this bitch ain't called the scrambler for nuthin'!"

Tabitha didn't really have a moment to collect herself. Raathe plopped her into a seat and dropped into the one next to her, grabbing his safety harness and securing it. Tabitha discovered her hands were shaking so badly she couldn't get her harness sorted and locked.

Caleb squatted in front of her, took the straps and straightened them and then locked them. "You ok, baby?"

Tabitha's chin wobbled. Sympathy made her resolve to be strong crumble faster than water could dissolve salt.

She nodded, unable to command herself to speak.

"Do not call her baby!" Raathe growled and swung at him, but the ship's rockets ignited at that moment and threw Caleb back into his seat—abandoned so that he could help Tabitha with her safety harness. He grabbed his harness and managed to secure one of the locks before the ship left the ground with a roar and enough drag to plaster all of them to their seats.

This boded ill for the artificial gravity, Tabitha realized even before they broke through the atmosphere some minutes later and into space and she felt her stomach try to crawl up her rib cage and turn inside out.

It was almost worse when artificial gravity abruptly kicked in.

As bad as she wanted to throw herself at the guys and feel their reassuring warmth, she had to wait until her stomach settled before she could even consider trying to get up.

Raathe unfastened her harness.

She thought for a couple of horrible moments that she was going to throw up on him, but she managed to overcome the nausea.

"You are sick?"

She couldn't shake her head. She was already too dizzy. "A little ill from the gravity transition," she responded, but she reached for him. She had to struggle with her tears when he enfolded her in his arms. There were no words to describe how wonderful it felt when she'd thought she would never feel his arms around her again.

He scooped her from the seat and headed toward the cabin area.

Appropriating the master cabin, he settled her on the bed and then lay down beside her and gathered her into his arms.

It flickered through her mind that she hadn't properly greeted Caleb or Korbin as she had Raathe, but she could only thoroughly engage them one at the time. They would just have to understand.

She hoped they would because she did care about them, very much.

But Raathe—well he was Raathe.

She was surprised but gratified when he made no attempt to initiate sex. He simply held her close as if he needed to feel her life as much as she needed to feel his.

"Why did you decide to leave the data stick for my … father?" she asked after a while, when she'd finally stopped shaking.

Raathe had been lightly stroking her back. At that, he paused. "Because he is your father. Because he is the grandfather of my child. In this way, neither of us need feel as if we had a hand in his death if it comes to that."

"You don't … hate me because of what he did?"

His arms tightened. "I do not think it is possible that I could ever hate you for any reason and I certainly would not for something that your father did or was involved in. This is why you were reluctant to come?" he asked.

It startled her and she lifted her head to try to read his expression. She found she couldn't pierce the darkness, however. She sighed and moved closer, squeezing him. "I wasn't reluctant. I just wanted to do what was best for the baby." It was only a partial truth, but it was certainly true.

"I didn't know you knew I hadn't decided whether to go with you guys or not."

"I have known you most of your life. I suspected."

She sighed. "I just wanted to do what was best for everyone," she said. "And I was worried I wouldn't be accepted if I came, but I knew you guys couldn't stay."

He was silent for several moments. "So … you have come because you know that we will be hunted if we try to stay in the human world?"

Pulling away, she slipped upward so that she was face to face with him. She lifted a hand to stroke his hard cheek. "You were always real to me and I always loved you. Now that I'm a woman—I just love you more. I came because I realized that life without you would be no life at all. Whatever comes, I'll be with you and that will make anything I have to face worth it."

He leaned toward her and pressed his lips to hers. At first, it was just a gentle pressure mouth to mouth, but the touch generated heat and want.

They made love in a leisurely fashion, slowly undressing one another, exploring one another as they never had before in their frantic couplings.

This was as exciting, as fulfilling, but more of bonding than ever before.

And, by the time they drifted to sleep in each other's arms, they had banished all lingering doubts and come together as soul mates.

Chapter Seventeen

Tabitha was certain when she felt the bed dip that it was Raathe leaving. She felt coolness on her side where he had been sleeping.

Confusion flickered through her when he filled the spot she thought he'd just vacated.

It took an effort, but she managed to pry one eyelid up to look.

Caleb's blurry face came into view. "Good morning, baby," he murmured, dipping his head to nuzzle her neck.

She groaned. "It's morning?" she asked weakly.

"More or less."

She didn't know whether to laugh or punch him out.

Clearly she hadn't been out a full eight or he wouldn't have said 'more or less'. "Damn it! I'm tired."

"We'll just snuggle then."

She knew better.

But she'd just spent a week weeping over his death. As tired as she felt at the moment she needed to show him how glad she was that he wasn't dead. "Well … ok. I missed you. I'll enjoy snuggling."

He said nothing for several moments, simply holding her and slowly stroking her back, but she noticed he was getting closer and closer to caressing her, edging closer to the side of her breasts and stroking down her ass to cup a cheek.

He'd just nibbled his way up her throat to her lips and covered her mouth with his when Tabitha felt the bed dip behind her. A few moments later, a hand snaked around her waist from that direction. And then he moved up close enough to wedge his cock between the cheeks of her ass.

Caleb apparently noticed they had company. He broke the kiss and levered upwards on one elbow.

Korbin planted a palm against his forehead when he did and gave him a shove that rolled him right out of the bed. Gathering Tabitha to him as Caleb hit the floor, Korbin smothered her protest beneath a fiery kiss and sent a wave of heat rolling through her.

"I'm so glad you're ok," she murmured, rubbing her face against his when he broke the kiss. "You didn't get hurt when we escaped?"

"No new holes," he assured her.

She tightened her arms around him. "Oh, baby! I'm so sorry you were hurt because of me!"

He shook his head. "Your father. We'll talk later."

Guilt still smote her. She knew she wasn't her father's keeper and he certainly didn't give a shit about her opinion of him, but she hated the association.

He distracted her by scooting down to find a nipple to

chew on.

Caleb plopped on the bed and rolled her toward him as Korbin leaned down and Korbin ended up with the nipple on his side while Caleb claimed the one closest to him.

Tabitha grabbed a fistful of hair on both heads and arched her back to offer herself to them, groaning as the pleasure of their mouths knocked the breath from her.

Korbin grabbed one thigh and dragged it toward him.

Caleb grasped the other and rolled between her legs.

Korbin let go of his nipple long enough to punch Caleb on the jaw and send him rolling off onto the floor again.

Caleb bounded up almost before he'd landed.

Tabitha put a hand on Korbin's chest and lifted one toward Caleb.

"If you'll stop, I'll give both of you a treat," she murmured in a husky voice, struggling to think of a position that might work.

They froze, staring one another down for a long moment with a cur dog look before transferring their attention to her.

She got the impression that they would have been just as happy to beat one another senseless, but the lure won out.

Needless to say, she'd never tried anything particularly kinky—certainly not a three way. She wasn't certain it was something she wanted to do now, but she *was* certain that she wanted to make peace.

It finally occurred to her after they settled on either side of her that—even though she'd never done a ménage—because human men were far more territorial than the cyborgs in that sense—she'd had a boyfriend that loved doggy and one that had pestered her constantly for oral sex. Those two positions, she thought, would work and very likely be novel to both—or at least Korbin.

She ran a hand along both of them from chest to groin. "You're overdressed," she murmured.

Both of them bounded up and stripped.

Poor Korbin got his shirt hung on his head—because he missed several fasteners—and ended up ripping it off.

While he was preoccupied with freeing himself, Caleb dove onto Tabitha and worked on revving her engines with his mouth and both hands. When he came up for air, Korbin planted a hand on his forehead and gave him a shove that sent him rolling toward the edge of the bed. That time he managed to catch himself. He balled his hand into a fist and drew his arm back, but then glanced at Tabitha and lowered it.

Korbin rolled over her as Caleb had, fastening a mouth to a breast and elbowing Caleb in the face when he leaned down to capture the other.

The nipple tweaking almost seemed more effective for the on again off again stimulation. Tabitha was warming up despite the sparring going on over her. She decided to see if she could redirect the guys to something a lot more pleasurable than punching each other in the face and reached out to stroke her hands over their chests and bellies.

She didn't know about them, but that excited the hell out of her. They felt fabulous.

And then she found the roots and shook hands.

That completely got their attention. Both of them stilled while she stroked their cocks and gently massaged their balls.

That lasted all of five minutes and they began to move restlessly.

She didn't really make a decision, per se. Her desires led her to lift her ass for Caleb and blaze a trail down Korbin's belly to test the fit of his cock in her mouth.

He clawed the bed when she sucked on the knob experimentally.

Meanwhile, Caleb, who had been stroking her ass, decided to shove his face into it. Grasping her thighs, he spread them so wide she nearly collapsed on the bed.

Her inner thighs were screaming and shaking until he shoved his face in her ass again and dragged his tongue from her clit to the mouth of sex and shoved it in.

The nose was a little distracting, but the tongue was talented.

She was so focused on how good that felt Korbin began to move restlessly again and stiffened as if he meant to get up or turn over.

She grasped his dick in a double hand lock and began stroking to the same beat as Caleb had established.

She was rushing toward climax when he came up for air and decided to shove his cock into her instead—which almost shoved her over Korbin.

He withdrew to check his aim and Tabitha braced herself on her elbows so that she could push back when he lined up and shoved again.

Progress!

She focused on bringing Korbin off while Caleb was plowing deeper and when he hit bottom, she decided it was time to polish Korbin's knob.

It was so exciting she almost came as soon as he started moving restlessly beneath her, clawing at the sheets. She could feel that he was close, that he would reach crisis any second and it boosted her own heat level until she was teetering on the brink.

Caleb's shaky thrusts pitched her over the edge. She groaned as she started to convulse and the vibration of her mouth combined with some fairly frantic sucking as she came seemed to set Korbin off. He stiffened, grunted breathlessly as if he'd been punched in the stomach when he began to ejaculate.

The quaking muscles of Tabitha's climax pulled Caleb into rapture with her.

The intensity blew her mind. She'd had hard climaxes with all three of her men, but coming in sync with Caleb and Korbin was a cut above. She came so hard she felt like her heart stopped for a handful of seconds and when the convulsions finally calmed she descended into a semi-comatose rapture, collapsing on the bed and panting for breath.

There was nothing semi about Korbin and Caleb's bliss. They transitioned in a matter of moments from panting to snoring.

"Nice," Tabitha murmured happily and found a comfortable spot between them.

* * * *

The trip to their new world took almost as long as the trip from Earth to Destiny, despite the fact that Destiny was a border world on the very edge of space inhabited by humans. Very likely, that was for the same reason, too—evasive flight path to make certain that they weren't being followed.

The ship was barebones. There were no luxuries—like a food processor where all they had to do was to order from a menu. They had to actually cook their food and clean up afterward.

There was virtually no entertainment—beyond real, physical cards and ancient board games and a half dozen books made of paper that they had to handle very carefully if they didn't want to risk losing chunks of the book.

The truth was, though, that Raathe, Caleb, and Korbin needed the recovery time. They'd recovered sufficiently to act, to rush to rescue Tabitha. And they'd been fortunate enough not to collect anymore lead in the process, but there had been very little acting to their 'playing dead' when her father's gang had filled them full of holes. They had been extremely damaged and, even with the nanos they all had, damage that severe took a while to recover from.

That being the case, they were content enough the first week or so to laze around the ship and play card games.

Tabitha had been through hell herself and *she* didn't have nanos.

Beyond that, she blossomed alarmingly—or rather her belly did.

She'd already been changed enough by her pregnancy when she arrived on Destiny to make it as clear as a bell that she wasn't just imagining the guys had pumped her full of real, live semen. She really and truly was pregnant.

A fact her father would have been able to notice if he had actually paid her any attention. Instead, he was so focused on finding the data he needed to save his sorry hide ....

She put that from her mind. He had no part in her life forever more. She at least had the relief of knowing he was not directly responsible for any of the horrific things that had been done to maximize corporation profits—and actually to boost them above their competition in that field.

Raathe had treated him better than he deserved, but she was glad for it.

Now she felt no guilt or grief about leaving her father forever.

He had never cared about her. She'd spent her entire childhood trying to earn the affection she wanted so desperately and he had withheld it.

She supposed, given the things he had let slip over the years, that he really had loved her mother and he couldn't bear to look at her because she looked so much like the woman he had loved and lost.

Or maybe he simply hadn't bonded with her because she was nothing like him?

It didn't matter now.

She was having a baby of her own and she believed that her guys loved her.

At least as much as they were capable of feeling.

Which was a damn sight more than her father had been capable of!

The cyborg hunters—who'd been posing as rangers—Reese and Dallas spent a good bit of the trip going over the laws and restrictions of the cyborg nation and the benefits. They made every effort to describe the capitol city, but Tabitha, at least, still wasn't prepared for the actuality.

They landed at the port shortly after sunrise and were escorted first to the med center where all of them were checked out.

And Tabitha discovered that she'd 'blossomed' because she was carrying twins. A DNA scan revealed that it was two females and they were the daughters of Raathe and Caleb—a stunning discovery to say the least.

Thankfully, the guys were thrilled—even poor Korbin although he was not a father-to-be at the moment.

Astonishingly, the hospital staff was beyond thrilled. They were so excited the news spread through the city as if it was major news. Which, it was. Girls were in such short supply and high demand that just the fact that she was carrying two immediately elevated her status as a citizen.

And the fathers', of course.

She was in good health and the babies were, news that brought her a lot of relief.

Nothing helped regarding Raathe, though. They began to immediately run scans and discuss possibilities and scheduled his surgery for late afternoon.

Tabitha was all to pieces by the time they took him in, holding on by a thread until he couldn't see she was the next thing to babbling idiocy in her fear for him.

Fortunately for her sanity the surgery not only went well, it was performed at lightning speed. When the med techs came out, she thought it was to announce that they were going in to surgery—not that they were finished.

But so it was—a done deal and performed without complications.

Raathe was able to leave the following day.

He dragged Tabitha straight down to the land and licensing bureau and she, Raathe, Caleb, and Korbin made a contract of partnership to co-habit in a domicile to be determined at a later date.

And, to settle the living arrangements, they went to the land office next and petitioned for a land lot and temporary living quarters.

Everything was moving so fast, Tabitha was too shocked to take it all in, but after that first burst of activity, Raathe seemed content to head to the apartment they'd been assigned and rest before the next round of furious activity.

Thankfully!

Tabitha wasn't certain whether it was a difference in her weight due to the properties of the planet or just her pregnancy, but she discovered she didn't have as much energy as she was used to.

Of course, she had endured months of extreme stress and activity and those probably contributed, but whatever the case she was more than ready to slow down and pace herself.

They went out that evening to celebrate their new family unit at a popular restaurant and went home to sleep—which Tabitha wasn't at all sorry for.

The following day they found transportation and took a trip into the country to look at the land they had been granted to build on.

Tabitha rested—content just to study the beautiful landscape—while the guys rambled through the forested land and checked on views and elevations to determine the best placing of the structures they planned and garden and pasture.

Their new neighbors came by to introduce themselves and welcome them—well most of the family. The woman explained that her man, Jerico, was tending the children.

Tabitha was stunned but thrilled to discover that Bronte was as human as she was and also a baby doctor. Her men that had come with her, Gabriel and Gideon, headed off to join Tabitha's to discuss 'business'.

Bronte chuckled when Tabitha confessed she'd been worried about the babies getting the care they needed. "They aren't going to need a lot," she said wryly. "I got here because they were terrified about their babies and had no notion what to do with them—so they sent my men to kidnap me."

Tabitha gaped at her in horror. "Seriously?"

Bronte laughed at the look. "Yes and no. They came for my father—I just happen to have the same first initial and last name and we're both pediatricians. Anyway, I basically volunteered because I didn't know what they were there for. And I have *not* regretted it one moment!"

Tabitha smiled an agreement at that. "I suppose, technically speaking, my guys kidnapped me, but ...." She shrugged and chuckled. "The way they saw it was that they were rescuing me and, it turned out, they were." She paused. "What did you mean the babies weren't going to need much care?"

"Well this is a brave new world we have here. They *are* making babies, but the babies are half human and half cyborg and they're typically born with nanos to take care of illness and injury, and they develop very quickly—around twice as fast as humans."

"Oh," Tabitha said, trying not to sound horrified and disappointed. "I was ... actually looking forward to having babies to nurture."

Bronte patted her hand sympathetically. "You'll have time for that. I promise."

Chapter Eighteen

The statement wasn't exactly prophetic, but it certainly turned out to be true—especially for a first time mother who had spent zero time around infants before she had her own. Tabitha had spent what was left of her short gestation period acquiring as much knowledge as she could cram into her head and volunteered to help with the local infants whenever she was allowed, but she found out pretty quickly that she *still* wasn't prepared for motherhood.

That, she discovered, was something mothers only truly learned in the field.

They were still living in the apartment when the big day arrived—because Raathe wasn't about to take a chance on her having the babies on *his* watch and neither Caleb nor Korbin felt competent to handle the delivery either. So, although they all settled on a house design and site location fairly quickly and Raathe, Caleb, Korbin and the neighbors on either side of them worked like fighting fire to get the house built before the babies came—and succeeded—Tabitha didn't know until she'd delivered and they announced that it was ready for inspection and move in whenever she was.

She was delighted—and relieved. Bronte would be right next door!

The first few weeks were something of a nightmare for all concerned.

The guys hung over the baby cribs and made funny faces and sounds to entertain the infants, but went into a blind panic the moment they began to scream. They broke a trail between their house and Bronte's, racing over to get her each time the babies reached screaming fits until she finally managed to convince them that the babies were in perfect health and just needed attention—feeding, burping, change of diaper—entertainment for their boredom.

They could avoid the hysterical screaming if they would

attend the babies' needs in a more timely manner instead of panicking and getting hysterical themselves.

Raathe was outraged at the suggestion that his concern could be interpreted as hysteria!

He told Tabitha that he suspected Bronte had arrived under false pretenses and wasn't a specialist on babies at all.

She contained her amusement with an effort, but said she just couldn't agree. It wasn't Bronte's fault that they forgot all instructions the minute the babies started screaming. She thought they just needed to get used to being parents.

Thankfully, as time passed, they did.

They settled into their new home and their new role as parents as the weeks turned to months. Raathe's background in security earned him a job as a consultant. Up until he had arrived, the entire safety of the cyborg nation was military in nature, but his knowledge of security gave them a whole new layer of protection.

Tabitha was encouraged to focus on nurturing her off-spring since all children were regarded as national treasure and their successful ascent to adulthood and good citizenship would be the foundation of the success of the nation.

Since the vast majority of the cyborgs that had built the nation were soldiers and had not been given any sort of programming on courting or human sexuality, Caleb's advice was in high demand and he was able to contribute substantially to the family wealth.

Korbin's background in medical technology was put to use in the med center. Even though the cyborgs themselves rarely needed any medical help, there were humans among them who did and an expectation that more would eventually make their way there.

The door of opportunity was beginning to close, though.

Most of the cyborgs had found their way to the colony

and set about the task of living, loving, and building. There were still strays, they knew, who had not found their way 'home' and that was why the door had not closed—yet— but they were running out of time to make that commitment before the cyborgs brought their agents home.

For herself, Tabitha pitied them if they missed the opportunity. It was a colony and that meant comfort had to be worked for and wasn't as abundant as it had been in the life she'd had.

In point of fact, having been wrapped in extreme wealth her entire life, Tabitha was terrified for a brief time when she realized that she was no longer protected by that wealth.

But then she realized she was protected by her men and, better than that, loved. She was surrounded by family for the first time in her life.

She had all the love she could handle, and then some.

Nothing beat that.

* * * *

Feeling exquisitely mellow in the wake of a blissful release, Tabitha smiled at her unborn child's antics as she lay in Raathe's embrace in the aftermath of their second anniversary 'celebration'.

She'd had to curtail the activities she'd had in mind due to her advanced stage of pregnancy, but she'd been determined she was going to have sex! She was horny damn it! And all of the guys had been steering clear of her for weeks—as if one prick would make her explode like a punctured balloon!

Raathe definitely hadn't been too keen on having sex when she was so close to delivery, but she'd managed to convince him there was nothing to worry about. Korbin might be anxious for the arrival, but his baby boy was content to wait a while longer.

It occurred to her, though, that she might have miscalculated when she felt the first pain.

Gas, she told herself, snuggling closer to Raathe, struggling to think of something to distract herself from focusing on what felt suspiciously like contractions unrelated to sex.

"You know," she said, "there's something that I've thought about a long time that I wanted to ask you."

Raathe had been drifting, but at that she had his full attention. "What?"

"Promise me you won't get mad at me for asking?"

That put him on full alert. "I promise that I will try not to get angry."

That gave Tabitha pause. Did she really want to risk pissing him off on their anniversary? When she'd had such a very nice celebration?

It had bothered her a long time, though. "I've just been trying to understand why it is that you always get mad and punch Caleb when he calls me baby. I mean, I know you disliked him just at first, but you seem to get along with him most of the time."

He was silent for so long she'd just decided that he was really, really pissed off when he finally spoke.

"I wanted to kill him when I caught him fucking you—when you were still just a child," he said, keeping his voice even with an effort. "I guess it just enraged me all over again every time he called you baby because it was a reminder than I had failed you when you needed me. I had not protected you."

She'd had no clue it was anything that … deep that was clearly very painful to him. Guilt swamped her.

It was her fault.

All of it and she'd dismissed it as petty jealousy.

"I was seventeen, Raathe. I know that's technically still a child—even legally—but I hadn't been a child mentally for a long time. That was *my* decision.

"I went to someone to get a fake ID. I asked around the school until I found out about the brothel. I took Father's credits to pay for it. And I was the one that picked Caleb. He was an older model and I thought his experience would make mine better. The madam tried to convince me to pick a different model, but I just wanted Caleb.

"I'm sorry it made you feel so bad. But I was young and I did it as much to punish you for not wanting me as to punish Father for trying to control every aspect of my life."

"Please stop blaming yourself and Caleb. I'm the one to blame."

Raathe didn't respond for several moments. Finally, he lifted a hand to her cheek. "You did it to punish me?"

She felt ashamed even to admit it. "I was a spoiled, petulant child in that regard."

He shook his head. "You were never spoiled and never petulant. And you have no idea how difficult it was for me to turn you down—or how much it tormented me that I could not be what you wanted me to be."

"Next time he calls you baby, I will remind myself that he only got you because I could not take advantage— because I think I would have if I had been able to."

Tabitha smiled and turned her face into his palm to kiss it. "Good. I think he's finally learned not to call me that in your hearing, but I'm glad we got it into the open." She paused for a long moment. "Please don't be pissed off …."

Raathe looked at her in confusion.

"Well, I may have miscalculated a little," she confessed hesitantly.

"Miscal …. Tabitha!" he growled.

"You said you wouldn't be pissed off!"

"I did not …. Are you having the baby?"

"Maybe. Will you be pissed off if I say, yes?"

"Gods damn it!" Raathe bellowed, leaping out of the bed and grabbing his trousers. "Korbin! Get your ass in here! Tabby's having your baby!"

The End.

The following is a short excerpt of the upcoming
Madelaine Montague release.

Immortal Highlander

By

Madelaine Montague

Chapter One

Evangeline paused in the act of brushing her long, blond hair, studying her reflection in the mirror or, more specifically, the mark on her breast visible above the low neck of the black dress she'd chosen for the evening. As so often happened when she wasn't actually struggling to capture a lost memory, something teased at the back of her mind. She tried to open her mind to it in the hope that that little something wouldn't simply tease her this time, but it was as elusive as ever and after a moment a mixture of anger and depression replaced the hopefulness.

She was *never* going to remember!

Resisting the urge to hurl the brush in frustration, she set it down on the vanity and tugged the neck of her dress a little lower, studying the mark on her breast just above her heart with frowning intensity. The doctors had scratched their heads over it briefly and finally dismissed it as a birthmark. They'd put it down to a strange quirk of nature and pure coincidence that the raspberry mark looked like a stylized tattoo of a flame. It wasn't a tattoo or even a scar.

It had nothing to do with the life she couldn't remember.

Evangeline wasn't her name, not her *real* name. It was one given to her by a friendly nurse who thought it was a shame to refer to her as Jane Doe after she'd woken from her coma. She didn't even know how old she was, let alone her name or who she might have left behind in the life she'd had before.

The thought brought her attention to her reflection again and she moved closer to the mirror to study her face. They'd told her she was somewhere between twenty and thirty.

That really narrowed it down, she thought in disgust! Particularly since they'd conceded that she could be a very young looking thirty-five!

She'd never borne a child.

That much was a relief anyway. It had tortured her that she might have a child somewhere wondering where their mother had gone.

So, did no child mean that she had no man in her life? Surely, if she was twenty-something she would have? Was the love of her life grieving over her? Thinking she'd simply run off? Thinking she was dead?

Or was there some evil man in her past who thought he'd safely disposed of her?

A shiver traveled down her spine at the thought. There'd been no sign of foul play when she'd been found, no indication that anyone had tried to murder her. But what did they *really* know?

She couldn't remember anything. Why would she be lying naked in a snow bank if she hadn't been tossed from a car in that state?

They hadn't said it outright, but they'd hinted their suspicions that she'd tried to take her own life, that she'd simply wandered into the snow naked and lain down to die. She didn't believe that. It didn't *feel* right. It didn't feel true. In any case, why hadn't they found her clothes? She'd been miles from anywhere she might have discarded them. They hadn't found clothing anywhere near her.

Of course, she didn't suppose they'd looked all that hard.

It was the fear that someone might be looking for her to finish the job they'd started that had prevented her from making any attempt to find the life she'd had before. As badly as she wanted to know she'd decided it was safer to simply cling to the hope the doctors had given her that one day her memories would come back.

She hadn't remembered so much as a glimmer from her past, though, in the year since she'd been found.

Giving up the attempt to determine her age from the few, faint lines she could detect, she studied the face itself. The shape of her high, prominent cheekbones suggested at least a hint of native American heritage regardless of the fact that her hair was more blond than brown and certainly not even close to black—naturally blond. It was growing from her scalp that way and time had confirmed it even if not for the skin tones and the light sprinkling of freckles that had suggested it all along.

So—where had she gotten the bone structure from? Father? Mother? Grandparents? From whom had she inherited the strange aquamarine eye color that fell somewhere between blue and green?

The face was comfortingly familiar. It wasn't just that she'd grown used to it *since* she lost her memory. She hadn't felt like she was staring at the face of a stranger even when she'd first woken up to discover that her past was gone. It was her only link with that past, the only clue she had of her identity.

Someone was bound to recognize it eventually.

She hoped.

Pushing away from the vanity, she ignored the vague sense of dread that swept over her and smoothed her hands over the black dress, grimacing wryly over the quality of the fabric it was made of. It was pretty and she thought it was flattering to her figure but it certainly wasn't expensive—not on her salary!

She was tired of waiting. She was tired of being afraid. She wasn't going to hide anymore! Someone, somewhere knew who she was! For better or worse, she was going to take the bull by the balls and find out!

Grabbing the tiny purse she'd bought to match the dress and shoes, she checked the contents to make sure she had stowed the essentials for her excursion—ID, cash, a small hair brush and makeup for touch ups—and headed out of her tiny efficiency apartment.

It was hell traversing four flights of stairs in high heels, proof that heels definitely weren't something she was used to wearing, but she managed to make it to the ground floor

without mishap and exited the apartment building. Despite
the distressing thoughts that had buzzed in the back of her
mind while she primped for her 'date', a mixture of
anticipation and anxiety began pumping through her as she
stood at the curb glancing up and down the street hopefully
for any sign of a taxi. She'd just decided she should call
one instead of leaving it to chance when she spied a
familiar yellow cab coming her way. Lifting one hand to
flag him down, she stepped from the sidewalk and moved
between the cars parked there. The cab driver skidded to a
halt a car length past her. The annoyance on his face
disappeared as he stuck his head out the driver window to
look back at her.

"I almost missed you."

"No," Evangeline muttered under her breath, holding a
hand to her wildly beating heart at the fright he'd given her.
"You almost hit me."

"Where to?"

"I'm supposed to meet someone at Del Torro's at nine."

The cab driver glanced at his clock as he set the meter.
"You're going to be a little late," he said wryly. "It's nine
fifteen now."

Evangeline shrugged inwardly. "Hopefully, he'll still be
there." A flicker of irritation went through her despite her
attempt to shrug her tardiness off. She hadn't intended to
arrive early any of the time. The clubs were barely
beginning to fill at nine and she wanted to have the chance
to observe the man she was meeting before he could spot
her. If he spotted her right away, she wouldn't get that
chance.

Of course, he might be watching the door—in which
case she'd made a blunder in her calculations, but she'd
thought she had a better chance of achieving her goal if
there were more than a handful of people in the club when
she arrived.

Worry settled in the pit of her stomach as the driver set

the car in motion, pressing her against the back of the seat. She'd seen a picture of him, but it was a poor quality picture. Would she even recognize him?

She doubted *he* would have a problem. She'd made sure she posted a high quality picture of herself on the dating site. The only reason she'd done it at all was in the hope that somebody would recognize her.

She hadn't mentioned the mark. It was her ace in the hole for testing anyone claiming to know her and she wondered abruptly if she'd made the right decision about the dress. The low neckline exposed that mark for all to see. Should she have worn something else? Something that would hide it? Because no makeup she'd discovered would and she'd known that when she chose the dress.

In for a penny, in for a pound, she told herself. She'd posted her bio and picture on every dating site she could find and so far zilch. She'd gotten a flattering number of flirts, but not one of the men who'd asked her out had known her.

Mark Kindle didn't either and she wasn't sure, now, why she'd agreed to meet him.

Actually, she *was* sure. She was as tired of being a hermit as she was of waiting for memories that remained elusive. She'd decided it was time to make a new life if she couldn't recover the old one.

She wasn't getting any younger—however the hell old she was!

A flicker of relief went through her when the cab set her down outside the club. There was a respectable line waiting to get in. She was in luck—she hoped! It seemed to her that there was a lot less chance that Mark would spot her first if she entered with a group.

The throb of the music enveloped her as she entered. Instead of pausing to allow her eyes to adjust to the gloom inside the club, she followed the 'herd' inside and looked around for the lady's room. Her luck held. There was one near the front of the club and she ducked inside with barely a glance toward the bar where Mark had said he would wait for her.

She thought she'd seen him, however.

After pretending to primp, she followed several other women as they emerged and glanced toward the bar again. The man had his back to her, but he glanced toward the entrance, giving her a view of his profile. He looked a little heavier and a bit older than the picture, but the hair color was right and the height seemed to be and he was wearing the dark suit he'd told her he would be wearing.

She didn't see anyone else that seemed to fit the description she had. Deciding it must be Mark, she debated briefly and decided to stroll around the club for another vantage point. She didn't get any bad 'vibes' from his appearance or his body language, but she decided she wanted a better look at his face.

As she glanced around the now rapidly filling club for a vantage point, she made eye contact with a tall man propping against the back wall of the club. A jolt went through her accelerating her heartbeat so swiftly that a wave of dizziness went through her. For several moments, she stood frozen, too caught up in powerful currents of emotion to really assimilate any of them. It occurred to her, vaguely, to wonder if he was even looking at her, but she couldn't seem to command herself body to move at all. Finally, through sheer force of will, she managed to glance behind her. There were several people in the man's line of vision, she discovered, but failed to convince herself that she wasn't the object of his attention. When she glanced around again, the man had disappeared.

"Evangeline?"

The jolt that went through her that time was more easily recognizable. She whirled toward the man who'd spoken, stared at him blankly for a moment and finally managed to curl her lips in a facsimile of a smile.

"I'm Mark—Mark Kindle."

It was the man she'd spied at the bar, she discovered without much surprise but with a good deal of dismay. She smiled wider. "Mark! How nice to meet you—uh—in person! I don't know how I missed you when I came in."

His gaze scanned her length in an overall assessment. "Have you been here long?"

Evangeline waved her hand dismissively. "Not long. I had trouble finding a cab. Sorry I'm late."

To her relief, he accepted the social lie without displaying any skepticism. "Can I get you a drink?"

"Yes, thanks. Something fruity," she said trying to dismiss her discomfort.

He settled a hand on her elbow. "Why don't we find a table first while there's still a chance of getting one?"

He glanced away, scanning the club before she could reply, and then began to steer her toward an empty table as far from the dance floor and the origins of the music as he could get. It wasn't a quiet corner. She doubted there was one in the entire club, but that had been one of the reasons she'd agreed to meet him in a club to start with—the fact that the music would fill any uncomfortable voids in conversation. The other was the 'safety' such a public meeting afforded.

She still had mixed feelings about the table he'd chosen and watched him as he headed back to the bar for the promised drink with a touch of irritation. She'd been distracted by the stranger and caught before she'd had time to decide whether she actually *wanted* to meet Mark in person or not.

That thought effectively having brought the stranger back to the forefront of her mind, she glanced around for any sign of him, trying to analyze the barrage of emotions that had pelted her when she'd noticed him, wondering how he'd managed to disappear so thoroughly when she'd glanced around. The same sense of breathlessness assailed her as she resurrected the memory.

Attraction—definitely—and one powerful enough to knock her socks off if she'd been wearing any—a sense of danger.

She frowned. Why the sense of danger? He hadn't done a thing but stared at her intently.

Was that because he'd recognized her, she wondered, feeling a fresh surge of adrenaline? Or had he felt the same instant, powerful attraction?

Oh yeah! That could happen, she thought wryly, struggling to conjure a mental image.

Tall, dark, and rangy muscular with an angular face.

Not her type at all.

Ok, so she didn't actually know what her 'type' was and it was pretty hard to deny her reaction.

Had it been recognition on some level in her that had created the shock to her system, though?

As her eyes finally settled on a man moving purposefully toward her, she realized she might just be about to find out. It took an effort to resist the urge to leap to her feet and flee.

She tried to convince herself for several moments that the man wasn't moving toward her. That lasted right up until he pulled the chair out across the table from her and settled in it as if he'd been invited.

Disconcerted, she simply stared at him, struggling to think of a polite way to point out that she had a date.

His face was devoid of expression as he scanned her, his gaze speculative. It didn't linger long on her face, however. Her breasts seemed to have snagged his attention. She squirmed uncomfortably, struggling with the urge to cover the cleavage she'd been unwise enough to display. "Do I know you?"

The question brought his gaze to her face—thankfully. At least she thought she was relieved until she found herself staring into his eyes.

"I know you."

His voice was deep enough to send tingles of awareness through her. The timber of it and his strange, thick accent, distracted her for several moments. Excitement and fear both rushed through her when she finally assimilated what he'd said. "You know me?" she gasped before it dawned on her that his response had seemed to carry undertones. "What do you mean 'you know me'?"

His gaze flickered to her breasts again and she realized, contrary to the conclusion she'd instantly leapt to, there was no lust in his gaze. He was staring at the mark. A coldness swept through her. Unconsciously, she covered the mark with one hand. He met her gaze again.

"I have questions."

Evangeline's lips tightened. "Unfortunately, I don't have any answers," she responded tightly. "And my date is coming back."

He tilted his head, studying her speculatively for a long moment and then glanced around the club as if debating with himself. "We talk later," he said coolly, rising to his feet and sauntering off as coolly as he'd approached her to begin with.

Evangeline gaped at his back. "Not if I see you coming," she muttered finally.

He halted abruptly, almost as if he'd heard the comment. She knew he couldn't have. It wasn't as if she'd yelled it at him and the music was loud enough it made conversation difficult when anyone was directly beside one.

And yet he glanced back at her. "You won't."

Evangeline blinked, wondering if the comment she thought she'd heard was purely her imagination. Imagination or not, it sent an eerie feeling through her.

Mark, on his way back to the table with the promised drink, was glaring after the man, she discovered. He was still frowning when he reached the table. "A friend?"

Evangeline forced a smile. She was sorry she had when

she realized the question hadn't been an idle one. He looked miffed.

That was getting damned possessive in a damned big hurry!

The date was all downhill from there. Evangeline was inclined to think they wouldn't actually have clicked—on her side—even if not for the strange encounter, but that certainly didn't help a situation that was already more than a little awkward. Gritting her teeth, she stuck it out and struggled to find some common ground for conversation for a little more than an hour and finally fabricated the excuse that she had to work the following day.

He didn't take that social lie nearly as well as the first, but she managed to scrape him lose and climb into a taxi by herself with the promise that she'd email him the following day.

An excerpt from book two follows:

Cyberevolution Book Two

Total Recall

By

Kaitlyn O'Connor

Chapter One

Chloe had been studying the game board intensely for a while before the sound of the alert buzzer finally penetrated her absorption. Frowning, she lifted her head and turned to stare at the ship's console. It was the message alert annoying the shit out of her, she realized with more than a touch of irritation.

Struggling to tune the noise out, she returned her attention to the game and finally made her move. For a few moments she hovered over her decision and finally set the piece down and stood up. "Don't touch anything until I get back!" she said. "One of you cheated last time!"

Jared and Kane exchanged a long look.

"We were not programmed to cheat," Jared responded.

"You're sure Pops didn't tinker with your programming?" Chloe threw back at him. "Because that move looked a lot like something he would've done."

"Pops cheated?" Kane asked blankly.

Chloe turned and grinned at the two cyborgs as she reached the console and punched the button to silence the alert buzzer. "Don't tell me! He told you it was a new rule, right?"

Jared and Kane shared a glance.

"It was not?" Kane asked.

Chloe chuckled. "I knew it was you, Kane!"

His olive complexion darkened with a mixture of discomfort and anger—well, simulated, she reminded herself. She shook her head at herself. What did it matter, really? If they seemed real enough that she had to keep reminding herself that they weren't, then why do it?

Because she worried, that was why.

It had been different when her father was alive. Working as deep space salvagers, they spent a lot of time in space, just the two of them after her father's last two crewmembers quit. As her father often said, they kept each other sane. The loneliness of spending weeks or months in space without seeing another soul could fuck up a person's head if they didn't have someone to interact with.

She didn't know what she would've done if they hadn't picked up the two cyborgs, Jared and Kane, on Xeno-12. They'd been seriously fucked up at the time, horribly! Her father had been more inclined to leave them than to gather them up with the other salvage but, as it turned out, the cyborgs were the only thing they'd picked up that were worth anything. Most of what they'd collected had been so degraded by the frigid temperatures they'd had to sell it for scrap and they'd been damned lucky to get anything for it.

Jared and Kane—well, they'd 'recovered' amazingly enough—so well it was impossible to tell, looking at them now, that they'd been so damaged that they'd looked downright nightmarish. Even before they'd fully recovered, they'd proven they could pull their own weight as crewmembers. They *were* cyborgs, designed as soldiers, which meant they weren't much for conversation but then again the two crewmembers they'd replaced hadn't been either.

Truthfully, they were way better company than the two jerk-offs they'd replaced, worth their weight in platinum, especially after her father had died. She'd had reason to be grateful she'd talked her father out of selling them for scrap!

Shaking her thoughts before she could get caught up in her grief over her father, she turned her attention to the computer and pulled up the incoming message that had set off the alert. She'd been expecting junk mail since she didn't know anybody who would actually send her a personal message. She skimmed through the message the computer pulled up skeptically and with very little interest. The alert at the top caught her attention, however.

TOTAL RECALL! Attention all owners of cyborgs manufactured by Robotics, Inc. in the S-series. Due to a suspected defect in programming that could cause serious injury or death, Robotics, Inc. has issued a total recall of all units in this series. Consumers will be compensated and/or the unit replaced with a model of comparable value once the unit has been returned and processed. If you own a cyborg of the S-series, please return it to your nearest dealer at your earliest convenience, or if there is no dealer conveniently located near you, the nearest military facility, police station, or ranger outpost for collection. This recall includes all cyborgs shipped as soldiers, sexdroids, and med techs ....

"Whoa! Hey guys! You've been recalled!" Chloe said with a chuckle. "Says right here that you're defective."

Jared and Kane, she saw when she glanced at them, were staring at her blankly. They exchanged a long look and she chuckled again.

"I'll just file this in the trash. I think if either of you were defective I'd know it by now."

Punching the delete button, she hurried back to the game they'd been playing, studying the board suspiciously until she'd determined that all the pieces were just as they had been when she'd gotten up. Satisfied, she looked up at Jared. "Your move."

He stared at her for so long that she realized he'd actually been disturbed by the message—well, confused, maybe. It was hard to say exactly how their minds processed. They had AI besides their programming. Of course, the cyborgs sold as soldiers as these two had been weren't expected to interact socially on a very refined level. They didn't need to as soldiers, and she supposed, since that was all they were exposed to initially, that their 'personality' was pretty well established before she and her father had picked them up. They were 'born' soldiers and she doubted their AI was sophisticated enough for them to 'adjust' now to anything else.

Well, they worked just fine with the salvage operation, but that wasn't actually all that different than what they'd done before—except for the fighting, which wasn't something they had to worry about too much. Occasionally, they ran into pirates or rival salvagers and things could get hairy, but that was rare. They *had* encountered a nasty rival salvage operator since they'd taken the two cyborgs in, which had required the cyborgs' battle skills and was probably the only reason she was still alive. That was certainly the reason her father wasn't, but battle wasn't something they commonly had to worry about.

"Hey! Don't worry about it! I know you aren't defective. *I'm* not worried about it and it isn't like me and Pops bought you two, you know? They aren't going to have any records of a transaction. Of course, I guess we'll have to watch it when we get into port to sell the salvage, but we don't even have the hold half full. It'll be months before we hit another port and by that time this will all have blown over. And, if it hasn't—well, I'll just tell them you're crewmembers. No sweat. If I didn't know for a fact that the two of you were cyborgs, I'd never believe it. You can pass as human without any problems."

Jared glanced at Kane again, but then focused on the board. Chloe could see he was still tense, though. Searching her mind for something to redirect their minds, she suddenly thought about Damon.

It wasn't a particularly happy thought. She'd worked damned hard to put Damon out of her mind, but since he'd popped up, she figured, maybe, it would be a good thing to talk about. It would distract them and maybe it would help her to get it off her chest. It wasn't something she'd been able to talk about with her father and she didn't have anybody else.

"Say, did I ever tell you guys about my first?" she asked. She noticed when she glanced at them that she had their attention and she snorted faintly with a mixture of embarrassment and self-depreciation.

"Ok, so this is embarrassing—don't laugh! I was like—oh—twelve, I guess, maybe thirteen when mom was killed and they notified Pops so he could come and collect me from the juvenile holding facility. Anyway, I never quite got around to—doing it—you know?"

She saw when she glanced at them that they were staring at her blankly in confusion. "Sex," she clarified wryly. "I'd done a little messing around, but nothing much. Honestly, it was so awkward I wasn't really comfortable with it. Anyway, I didn't and I sure as hell wasn't interested in any of the other crewmembers on board the ship. Take my word for it! Total creeps and nasty! So one day Pops gets drunk as a coot and asks me about it. Mind you, I was twenty at the time, and he finally gets around to talking sex education!" She shook her head. "Good old Pops! I'd pretty much figured it all out by then, of course. I just hadn't had any experience. So I'm thinking Pops has forgotten all about it by the time we hit another port, but, hell no! The first thing he does after we've processed the salvage and collected our money is insist that the two of us need to head down to a brothel and get our pipes cleaned!"

She shrugged. "I wasn't really that comfortable about Pops suggesting it, but I wasn't against the idea. He'd pretty much convinced me when we had the talk before that I couldn't go wrong by going to a sexdroid the first time since they're just—well! Anyway, so we get to the brothel and there's this absolutely *divine* cyborg sexdroid named Damon! And he didn't just look yummy. He had all the right moves!

"I was stiff as a poker," she added, laughing. "But he knew exactly what to do and not only did it not hurt—at all—but it was …. Well, it was just wonderful! It wasn't at all like it was when I was a kid with the other kids. No slobbering or groping. He kissed dreamy and … everything else. I enjoyed myself so much I didn't want to leave," she said, chuckling. "I tried my best to talk the owner into selling him to me, but the dip-shit wouldn't go for it.

"Pops laughed his ass off that I'd gotten so … attached to him, but I sure as hell hated to leave him. Said I took to sex like a duck to water … whatever that is."

She hadn't expected it to depress her to tell them the story. She'd thought it was funny—sort of—and it would lighten the mood. There was no getting around the fact that it *had* depressed her, though.

"I was fully programmed to perform as a sexdroid," Jared said after a fairly lengthy pause.

Kane frowned at him when he said nothing else and finally turned to her. "I was also."

Chloe looked at both cyborgs with surprise. "No shit?"

"I am not shitting you," Jared assured her, his expression earnest. "It would not be difficult to access the programming, although I have not had occasion to use it before."

Chloe studied both cyborgs speculatively, discovering with more than a little surprise that she hadn't noticed how handsome they were. Not that they were as handsome as Damon, but they were a sight better looking than any man she'd ever seen—real man—not that she'd seen a lot since she was old enough to actually notice. There didn't seem to be many good looking men in the salvage business and the men at the bars—well, the best looking ones were usually pirates!

The weird thing was that she hadn't actually noticed Jared or Kane, not really. It didn't take a lot of searching to figure that out. It had been painful to look at them when they'd first recovered them. She'd gotten into the habit of *not* looking at them, not directly. She knew, of course, that they were amazingly tall and brawny. That sort of went with the territory, though. At least, she figured it did, that the company had gone out of their way to create soldiers that were intimidating in size alone. They didn't actually need to. They could've been half the size they were and they still would've been stronger and faster than any human counterpart, but they wouldn't have *looked* as intimidating.

Now that they'd drawn it to her attention, though, she actually studied them.

Jared was almost 'pretty boy' handsome in the face—without a sign of a scar despite the fact that most of one cheek had been missing when they'd pulled him off that frozen planet. It made her belly clench just remembering it.

His hair had grown, but she thought the shoulder length, dark hair sort of set off his almost classical features and, truthfully, she'd never liked the short hair the military favored.

Kane was more rugged looking, but attractive in a very manly way. With his black hair and olive complexion, he reminded her strongly of pictures she'd seen in her study data of the 'wild natives' discovered on the North American continent on Earth in ancient times.

For a handful of moments, she tried to imagine herself locked into the sort of embrace that she'd enjoyed with Damon, but although it stirred a lot of warmth—alright carnal heat—it also made her feel a little uncomfortable. Images wafted through her mind of Jared and Kane as they'd looked when her and her father had found them, though, and she abruptly knew why. One part of her knew they were just machines, that they couldn't *be* abused in the sense that a living thing could, and yet she had been so angry at their condition at the time—still was—and ashamed that their government was responsible for the horrors she and her father had seen. It made her feel guilty even to consider taking further advantage of them. It just wasn't right. She didn't care if they were supposed to be nothing but machines. They looked and acted human and that was enough to make the government's negligence heinous. In point of fact, there'd been human soldiers among them that had suffered the same fate, although she hadn't known it at the time. She didn't like to think about the incident—at all—because in the back of her mind she'd had this terrible fear ever since that they'd left someone that might have been saved if they'd only kept looking. She forced a chuckle. "Hey! Thanks, guys, but don't access it on my account! I'm pretty sure I've got zero sex drive. I hadn't even thought of having sex since …."

Chloe broke off abruptly as a sudden thought hit her like a rogue meteor. Her eyes widened and she jolted up from her chair, upsetting the game board in the process. "Oh my god! Damon! Total recall! Oh my god! That means they'll be recalling Damon! He's an S series. I'm sure he was!"

She tried to tell herself that it wasn't likely that they really meant to recall *all* of the cyborgs, but panic gripped her and she couldn't shake the thought that he was even now being packed up to be shipped back to the company. "He wouldn't let them take Damon," she muttered to herself as she dashed to the ship's console. "Damon was the only male sexdroid the proprietor had. He wouldn't let *me* buy him, damn it! There's no way he'd turn him over."

She glanced toward Jared and Kane. "What do they do when they recall cyborgs—droids?"

Jared's lips had formed a tight line. "Disassemble."

"*Disassemble!*" Chloe practically shouted. "Oh my god! Well, I've got to go after him! That's all there is to it!"

Her hands were shaking when she pulled up a map and began to search for Thagorous. "System, system …! Shit! I can't remember the name of the god damned system! Shit! Shit! Shit! Computer! Bring me up a list of planets named Thagorous and their star systems!"

"You are going there?"

Chloe threw a distracted glance in the general direction of the voice and realized both Jared and Kane had followed her. "Of course I'm going there … wherever …. That's it! The Medaly Galaxy, Osirus system! Computer! Calculate a jump to this coordinate."

"From what point of origin?"

"This point you dumb shit!" Chloe snapped. "Honest to god! Computers and their stupid questions." She glanced up at Jared and Kane a little self-consciously. "I meant the computer-computer, not you guys."

"Why are we going there?" Kane asked.

Alright. So Kane could be pretty fucking dense! "Damon?"

"We cannot make that jump," Jared said tightly.

"From this point of origin, it would require three jumps," the computer announced.

"I don't care how many fucking jumps it would take, damn it! Didn't I just say calculate it?"

"This is not reasonable," Kane growled.

Chloe turned and gave him a look. "Not reasonable? Didn't you *hear* what I said?"

"You wish to extract Damon, a sexdroid, before his owner can return him to the company and we are three jumps from the coordinates where you last knew him to be," Jared said.

Chloe stared at him. That was, quite possibly, the most she'd ever heard him say at one time. "So?"

"The ship is old. It would be dangerous to attempt three jumps in succession. Beyond that, the droid you refer to may not even be in the possession of the brothel where you first ... utilized his services. This incident you referred to—how many years, Earth standard, since it occurred?"

"This is a *hell* of a time to decide to be talkative!" Chloe snapped. "Damon's in trouble! I can't just let them tote him off and disassemble him!"

"He is not yours," Jared said pointedly. "This is not your decision. If he has been recalled you would not be able to purchase him from the owner even if he still had the cyborg in his possession. In all likelihood, by the time you could reach this system, he will have been turned over to the authorities and you will not be able to convince them to give him to you. I do not understand why this cyborg is important enough to you to expend so much fuel and take unnecessary risks."

Chloe felt her face reddening. "You wouldn't understand if I tried to explain it," she muttered. "I'll worry about how to get him out of this mess when I get there. I have to know what I'm dealing with, after all, before I can make plans. It's an out-of-the-way system. They might not have heard and even if they had, the proprietor wasn't keen on giving him up. He could still have him. Just ... get the ship ready, alright? And then get into the harnesses. I don't want you two splattering against the bulkhead when we make the jump—jumps. You'll knock a hole in it." Dismissing them, she returned her attention to the ship's navigational computer. "Prepare for the first jump. When we emerge, run a thorough system's check, recalculate the second jump—just to be sure your calculations from here aren't off—and then take the second. Repeat that process before you take the ship through the third jump. Understood?"

"Affirmative, Captain Chloe."

"How many hours away from the target planet will we be when you've taken the third jump?"

"Estimated 8:34:20 Earth standard."

Chloe chewed her lip. "That's getting us as close as you can with the third jump?"

"Affirmative. The third jump will place the exit from folding just beyond the last planet of the Osirus star system. I do not have the data to execute a jump within the system."

"Fuck! Well, it'll have to do, I guess, if it's the best we can do! Give us fifteen minutes to lock down before you execute the first jump."

"Countdown ... mark. Fifteen minutes ...."

Chloe bumped into Jared when she shot out of her seat. She would've ricocheted off of him and hit her seat again except that he caught her on the rebound. She gaped up at him. "What are you two standing there for? Look alive, guys! Let's get this bucket of bolts locked down for a jump!"

"This is a dangerous undertaking. I do not understand your reasoning. I am fully capable of fulfilling your needs as a sexdroid ... as is Kane. If you had only mentioned this before, I would have taken care of your needs. This is completely unnecessary."

Chloe merely stared at him for a moment. Slowly, it dawned on her as she studied their set, angry faces that they weren't just confused. They were ... disturbed. Maybe because they felt threatened in some way? She patted Jared's arm. "Hey! You two guys are my best buds! No way am I going to let the bad old company men get their hands on you! Don't sweat it! I'll leave you two on board while I head down to the planet to grab Damon." She pulled away from him. "Now let's get everything stowed for the jump!"

Jared glanced at Kane as she swept past them, hurrying to grab up the game board and pieces. "We will check the load in the hold," Jared said finally.

"Good idea!" Chloe said absently, rushing around the bridge, grabbing things up at random and tossing them into the lockers. "When you've checked it, do a cabin check."

"The load is secure," Kane growled when they had left the bridge. "Why did you say that we would go and check it when we *know* it is secure!"

Jared slid an irritated glance at him. "I did not want her to hear the discussion," he retorted testily.

"What discussion? How will it help for us to discuss this? We must reason with her! I do not know why she is determined to go to this place, regardless of the danger, only to retrieve a sexdroid—particularly when we can do as well!"

"I do not understand either. I thought you might," Jared said tightly. "What do you suppose she meant when she said that we were her 'best buds'?"

Kane frowned. "This is slang for friendship—between two males."

"This is what my reference says, also. But she is not a male! She is confused and believes herself to be male? Or she is confused and believes us to be female?"

"She is disturbed over this gods damned sexdroid!" Kane growled. "She is not behaving at all rationally."

"I think I have been insulted," Jared said after mulling it over. "If she meant companion, then I am not insulted, but if she is thinking that I have no sexual significance because she believes I am a friend, then I am definitely insulted! She cannot have meant that she cannot consider us as sexual partners because we are cyborgs, for she stated very clearly that this Damon is also a cyborg."

"You are not more insulted than I am!" Kane snapped. "Mayhap she did not believe that we truly have been programmed as sexdroids and she thinks that she must get this other cyborg for that reason?"

"Why would she not believe? She does not know that we are different now and that we *could* lie if we wished to!"

Kane lifted his head and stared at the door to the bridge, pondering the problem. "Mayhap we should show her? I have been thinking about it for some time now."

"You also?" Jared asked, clearly surprised. "How long?"

Kane frowned. "Why does that matter?"

"I was only wondering if you had completed the change."

Kane narrowed his eyes at him. "You are suggesting that I have not? Or that you are more advanced?"

Jared shrugged. "This is not the time to concern ourselves with such things! We should focus on thinking of an argument to convince her she does not need this god damned sexdroid! There is nothing that he is capable of that we are not also capable of. Mayhap we should ask her to detail what he did to please her and then convince her to allow us to demonstrate so that she can see we are as proficient in performing the same acts as he?"

"We could override the main computer and then show her that we are fully functional and capable of all the things the pleasure droids are," Kane said somewhat hopefully.

"She will *know*, then, that we are also rogues and she will turn us over to the company!"

"Well! I am not keen on collecting this gods damned sexdroid! *Then* she will fuck him and not us!"

"I do not believe I care for that possibility!" Jared said decisively. Turning, he stalked back onto the bridge, waiting until he had caught Chloe's attention. "Captain Chloe," he said, saluting her. "I would like to volunteer for the duty."

Chloe stared at him blankly. "What duty?"

"I will access my pleasure droid programming and fuck you whenever you feel the need for sexual relief."

Chloe's jaw slid downward until her mouth had formed an O of surprise. She blinked at him a few times and finally smiled. Jared had just begun to relax fractionally when she chuckled. "Oh, that's so sweet! I don't really need to fuck right now, ok? We'll talk about it later. Run along and secure the load, now."

Jared frowned but, try as he might, he could not think of another argument likely to sway her. Saluting again, he returned to the corridor where Kane was waiting.

"You convinced her?"

"I do not think so," Jared said slowly.

"Well! What did she say?"

"That she did not need to fuck right now."

Kane considered that. "But she is considering it?"

"She did not seem to be against the idea," Jared said finally. "She said we could talk about it later."

"But she did not cancel the jump?" Kane said tightly.

Jared shrugged. "Short of taking over the ship—which might alert the very people we wish to avoid—I see no hope for it since it seems we cannot persuade her. We will pick up the sexdroid and then we will dispose of the fucking bastard."

Made in the USA
Columbia, SC
13 February 2019